PAWS

PRIYA PUTS HERSELF FIRST

MICHELE ASSARASAKORN
NATHAN FAIRBAIRN

RAZORBILL

An imprint of Penguin Random House LLC, New York

First published in the United States of America by Razorbill,
an imprint of Penguin Random House LLC, 2023

Visit us online at PenguinRandomHouse.com.

Library of Congress Cataloging-in-Publication Data is available.
ISBN 9780593351963 (hardcover)
1 3 5 7 9 10 8 6 4 2
ISBN 9780593351970 (paperback)
3 5 7 9 10 8 6 4 2

Manufactured in China

TOPL

Illustrated by Michele Assarasakorn
Written, colored, and lettered by Nathan Fairbairn

Edited by Christopher Hernandez
Design by Maria Fazio

Text set in CCJoeKubert

We acknowledge the support of the Canada Council for the Arts.

Canada Council for the Arts Conseil des arts du Canada

This one is for Rachel.
My home is wherever you are.

—N. F.

For Nicko.

—M. A.

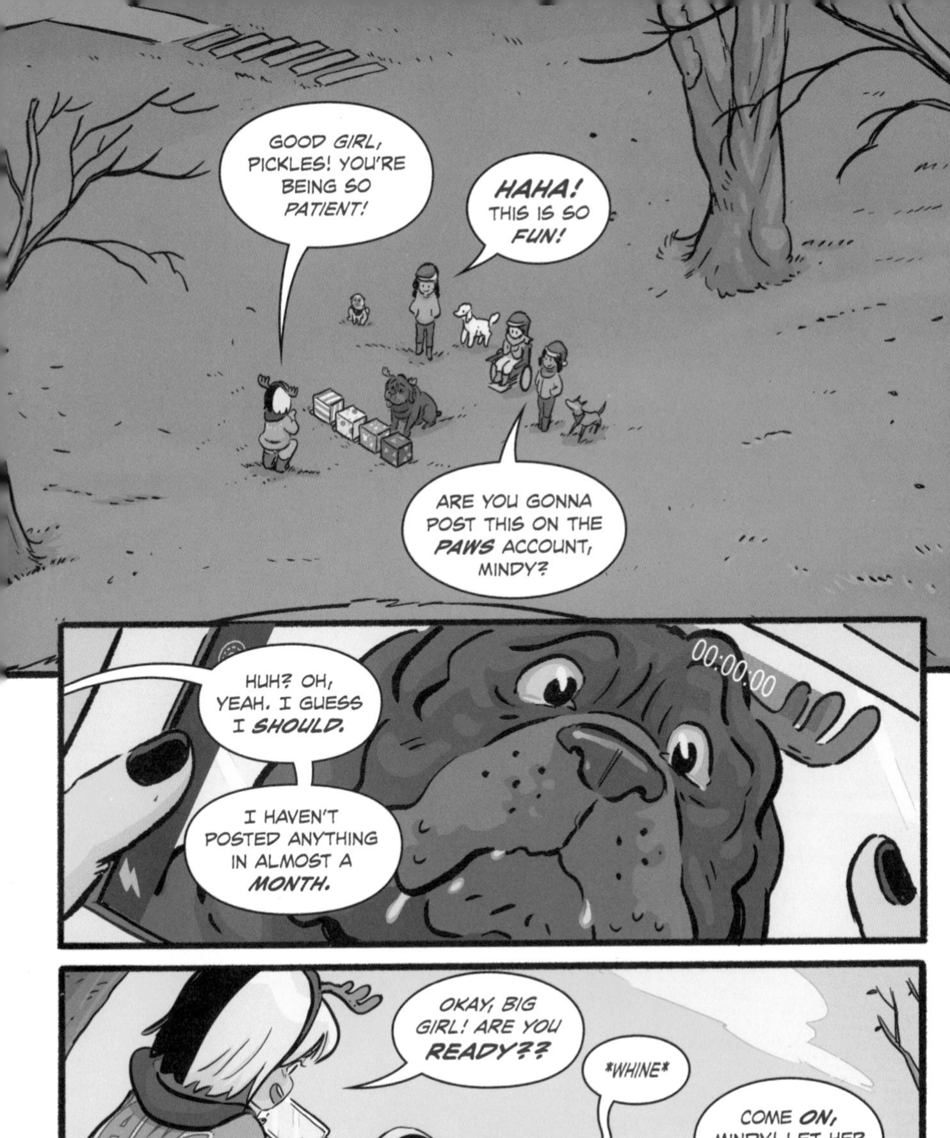
GOOD GIRL, PICKLES! YOU'RE BEING SO PATIENT!
HAHA! THIS IS SO FUN!
ARE YOU GONNA POST THIS ON THE PAWS ACCOUNT, MINDY?
00:00:00
HUH? OH, YEAH. I GUESS I SHOULD.
I HAVEN'T POSTED ANYTHING IN ALMOST A MONTH.

OKAY, BIG GIRL! ARE YOU READY??
WHINE
COME ON, MINDY! LET HER GO ALREADY!
PAWS

HAHA! OKAY, FINE!
GO AHEAD, GIRL! PICK ONE!

ARF!
BMP!
SNUFF!!
GOOD JOB, PICKLES!
YOU SNIFFED OUT THE BOX WITH THE BONE!!

HAHA!
THAT WAS AWESOME!

WHO'S NEXT?!
I THINK CARL IS INSISTING THAT IT'S HIS TURN!
ARF!

OKAY, NOW SIT, CARL.
SIT!

GOOD BOY!
WHINE

HOLD, CARL!
HOLLLLD...

GO!
ARF!!

CARL, NO!
JUST ONE GIFT EACH!!
HAHAHA!!

CARL! YOU GET BACK HERE WITH THOSE!
HI, THERE! MY NAME IS PRIYA GUPTA!

AND THESE ARE MY BEST FRIENDS...
MINDY PARK AND GABBY JORDAN!
A FEW MONTHS AGO, WE STARTED UP A DOG-WALKING SERVICE IN OUR NEIGHBORHOOD CALLED PAWS.
IT'S BEEN SO MUCH FUN, BUT ALSO A TON OF WORK, ESPECIALLY FOR ME!
MY FREE TIME WAS ALREADY PACKED WITH SPORTS EVEN BEFORE PAWS, SO IT'S BEEN ALMOST IMPOSSIBLE TO FIND TIME FOR BOTH! NOT THAT I'M COMPLAINING! I'VE BEEN KEEPING IT TOGETHER OKAY SO FAR...
...ESPECIALLY SINCE OUR NEW FRIEND HAZEL JOINED PAWS LAST MONTH.
SHE'S REALLY PICKED UP MY SLACK!
IT'S BEEN A WILD YEAR, AND IT'S NOT OVER YET!
I CAN'T WAIT TO SEE WHAT HAPPENS NEXT!

LATER...
CHANCE CAFE
Merry Christmas!
CHANCE CAFE
OPEN!
Bubble Tea, Baos, Coffee!
COME ON IN!
I CAN'T BELIEVE CHRISTMAS IS ONLY THREE DAYS AWAY!
I KNOW!

CHRISTMAS IS GREAT, BUT FOR ME THE BEST PART IS NO SCHOOL FOR TWO WHOLE WEEKS!
NOTHING TO DO BUT LIE AROUND AND CHIIIIILLLL.

I'M PUMPED TO SEE MY GRANDPARENTS! I HAVEN'T SEEN THEM SINCE MOVING HERE.
THEY'RE GOING TO BE STAYING WITH US FOR THE WHOLE BREAK!

PFFT! WHAT'S WITH YOU GUYS? I'M LOOKING FORWARD TO ONE THING AND ONE THING ONLY--
PREZZIES!

OH! AND DAD'S CHRISTMAS DINNER!
AND ALL OF THE BAKING MY MOM AND I DO!
AND ALL THE CANDIES LYING AROUND AT ALL TIMES!
AND HOLIDAY MOVIES! AND--

HAHAHA!
OKAY, GABBY! WE GET IT!
HOW ABOUT YOU, PRIYA?
WHAT ARE YOU MOST LOOKING FORWARD TO?

OH, I DUNNO. I GUESS JUST OPENING THE PRESENTS YOU GUYS GAVE ME?
I'M NOT REALLY AS WILD ABOUT CHRISTMAS AS GABBY!

OH! IS THAT BECAUSE YOU'RE FROM...UH...
INDIA? I THINK?

HAHA, YEAH, I GUESS SO.
CHRISTMAS IS A PRETTY RECENT DEVELOPMENT IN MY HOUSE, THAT'S FOR SURE.

OH, THAT MAKES SENSE.
SORRY, I GUESS I SHOULD HAVE KNOWN THAT.
HA! IT'S OKAY. DON'T SWEAT IT.
IT'S NOT LIKE I EVER REALLY TALK ABOUT IT.

"WE MOVED HERE FROM INDIA WHEN I WAS *REALLY* LITTLE.
MY PARENTS ARE HINDU, LIKE MOST PEOPLE IN INDIA, SO WHEN THEY GOT HERE THEY DIDN'T DO *ANY* CHRISTMAS STUFF AT ALL.
YVR
YVR
International Arrivals
Arrivés internationales
Welcome to
Bienvenue au
Canada

BUT ONCE I WAS IN SCHOOL, I FELT KINDA LEFT OUT (AT LEAST, THAT'S WHAT MOM SAYS-- I DON'T REALLY REMEMBER), SO WE STARTED TO CELEBRATE IT A LITTLE BIT.
GLUE

EVERY YEAR THEY GET A LITTLE MORE *INTO* IT!
AT FIRST, THERE WAS MAYBE A COUPLE LITTLE DECORATIONS AND I ONLY GOT ONE GIFT...

...BUT NOW MY LITTLE BROTHERS GET A *REAL* TREE AND STOCKINGS AND THE WHOLE *DEAL!*"
Ajit
Priya

OH, THAT'S WEIRD. I ALWAYS ASSUMED THAT YOUR PARENTS TOTALLY *LOVED* CHRISTMAS!
THEY ALWAYS PUT YOUR LIGHTS UP SO *EARLY!*

THOSE LIGHTS AREN'T FOR *CHRISTMAS,* YOU GOOF!!
THEY'RE FOR *DIWALI!!*
DI-WHAT-I?

OMG, IT'S LIKE THE *MAIN* HINDU FESTIVAL! IT'S THE FESTIVAL OF LIGHTS! IT'S BASICALLY THE ONLY TIME ALL *YEAR* WE GO TO TEMPLE.

TEMPLE?
IS THAT LIKE CHURCH?

YEAH, KINDA. TO BE HONEST, I DON'T *LOVE* IT.
WE DON'T REALLY *KNOW* ANYONE THERE, AND THEY ALWAYS HOLD SERVICES IN *HINDI...*
WHICH IS ROUGH BECAUSE MY HINDI IS PRETTY *BASIC.*

HAHA!! THAT'S KINDA LIKE ME!
THE ONLY TIME I'VE EVER BEEN TO CHURCH IS FOR CHRISTMAS MASS! MY NANA DRAGS ME THERE WITH MY MOM AND MY AUNTIES.
I THINK MY DAD LIKES IT BECAUSE HE AND MY GRANDDAD GET TO STAY HOME TOGETHER AND DRINK EGGNOG.

WHAT?! WHY DON'T THEY HAVE TO GO WITH YOU?
MY MOM WOULD LOSE IT IF DAD DIDN'T COME TO CHURCH WITH US ON SUNDAYS!

HM, DAD DOESN'T BELIEVE IN ANY OF THAT STUFF, BUT I'M NOT SURE WHY GRANDDAD DOESN'T GO.

WAIT, DID YOU JUST SAY YOU GO TO CHURCH ON SUNDAYS, HAZEL?
WELL, I USED TO, BACK IN CALGARY.
MOM'S STILL LOOKING FOR A NEW CHURCH HERE.

OH, I REMEMBER WHY GRANDDAD DOESN'T COME! HE'S JEWISH!
WHOA, YOUR MOM'S MOM IS CATHOLIC AND HER DAD IS JEWISH?
I DIDN'T KNOW LITERALLY ANY OF THIS.
Flourist

HAHA! HAVEN'T YOU ALL BEEN FRIENDS SINCE LIKE GRADE TWO?
HOW ARE YOU JUST FINDING THIS STUFF OUT NOW?

I DUNNO! IT JUST NEVER CAME UP, I GUESS!

HAHAHA! MY MOM IS ALWAYS COMPLAINING THAT KIDS NEVER TALK ABOUT ANYTHING PERSONAL.
SHE SAYS WE KNOW MORE ABOUT SOME RANDOM U-TUBER THAN WE DO ABOUT OUR OWN BEST FRIENDS.
WELL, YOU'D BETTER NOT TELL HER ABOUT THIS LITTLE CONVO, THEN.
OMG, CAN YOU IMAGINE?! WE'D NEVER LIVE IT DOWN!
RIGHT?!?!
HAHAHA!
CAFE

SOON...
MOM! I'M HOME!

<OH, HELLO, DEAR! DID YOU HAVE A NICE WALK?>*
yoghurt
*TRANSLATED FROM HINDI

YEAH, IT WAS *HILARIOUS!* WE GAVE ALL OF OUR DOGS THEIR PRESENTS AND IT WAS PURE ***CHAOS!***

CHUTKI, PLEASE COME INTO THE KITCHEN TO TALK.
<ALSO, I'D LIKE YOUR HELP WITH DINNER.>
OIL

GROAN

OKAY! BE RIGHT THERE!
HEY!
PRIYA! STOP! I CAN'T SEE!!

HEHEH! COMING, MOM!

PLEASE DICE THESE TOMATOES FOR ME.
OKAY. IS THIS FOR A MASALA?
YES, EXACTLY.

SO, YOU ARE FINISHED DOG WALKING UNTIL AFTER CHRISTMAS, YES?
YUP! NO DOGS OR SCHOOL OR SPORTS FOR THREE WHOLE DAYS!
CHOP CHOP

I AM HAPPY FOR YOU!
‹YOU'VE BEEN WORKING SO HARD THESE LAST FEW MONTHS!›
RIGHT?! I PLAN ON--

DEEDLE! DEEDLE DEET!
OH!

⟨OH, IT'S THE LANDLORD. I NEED TO TAKE THIS. SORRY, LOVE.⟩
THAT'S OKAY, MOM!

HELLO? OH, YES, HELLO, MELISSA. HOW CAN I HELP YOU?

WH-WHAT?

MOM?
WHAT'S GOING ON?

MOM?!

CHRISTMAS MORNING!
WHEN ARE THEY GONNA BEEE HERE?

GABBY, IT'S 8:30 IN THE MORNING!
NANA, GRANDDAD, AND AUNTIE CATH SAID THEY'D BE HERE AS SOON AS THEY GET UP AND DRESSED.
UGH!

WELL, HOW LONG IS THAT GONNA BE? I'VE BEEN UP FOR TWO HOURS ALREADY!
THUMP!

YES, I AM WELL AWARE...

I JUST GOT A TEXT FROM NANA. SHE SAYS THEY'RE ON THEIR WAY NOW--
AND THAT THEY'LL PICK UP CATH ON THE WAY.
WHICH MEANS THEY'RE STARTING TO GET READY TO LEAVE NOW.

BUT THAT'LL TAKE SO LONG!
CAN'T I OPEN JUST ONE PRESENT BEFORE THEY GET HERE?

WELL...
MAYBE WE SHOULD GIVE... IT TO HER BEFORE EVERYONE ELSE ARRIVES.
YEAH, OKAY. GOOD IDEA.

HEEHEE HEE!
"IT"?

MERRY CHRISTMAS!
OOOHH!!

THIS IS FROM YOUR MOTHER AND ME. IT'S YOUR *BIG* GIFT THIS YEAR, SO DON'T JUST--

WHATISITWHATISITWHATISIT WHATISITWHATISITWHATISITWHATISIT WHATISITWHATISITWHA--

OH.
MY.
GOSH.

I-IT--IT'S A...
PHONE.

OKAY, BEFORE YOU GET TOO EXCITED, I WANT YOU TO KNOW THAT THERE ARE GOING TO BE PLENTY OF RULES AND RESTRICTIONS ON THIS.

STARTING WITH NO PHONE USE AFTER 8 P.M.
AND NO PHONES IN YOUR BEDROOM AT NIGHT.
AND NO PHONES AT ALL DURING SCHOOL.

IT'S REALLY JUST FOR SAFETY WHEN YOU'RE OUT WALKING THE DOGS, AND--
GABBY? IS EVERYTHING OKAY? YOU'RE AWFUL QUIE--

YEE...

...EEEEEEESSSSSSS!!!

HUH. THAT'S WEIRD.
I THOUGHT I HEARD GABBY FOR A SECOND THERE.

OKAY! BREAKFAST IS SERVED!

SMELLS SO *GOOD!*

WHAT IS THIS, AGAIN?

IT'S AN OLD FAMILY TRADITION. WE HAD IT EVERY YEAR WHEN I WAS GROWING UP.
TO ME, THIS IS WHAT CHRISTMAS MORNING TASTES AND SMELLS LIKE.

YEAH, OKAY, BUT WHAT'S IT *CALLED?*

UM, "WIFE SAVER."
EX*CUSE* ME?

I *KNOW!* IT'S A BAD NAME! I TOLD YOU IT'S AN *OLD* RECIPE!
I GUESS THEY CALLED IT THAT BECAUSE IT SAVED THE WIFE TIME, BUT MY *DAD* WAS ALWAYS THE ONE WHO MADE IT.

ANYWAY, IT'S *REALLY* GOOD.
PLEASE *TRY* IT!

HMMM...

WELL?

YUM!!
HOW DO YOU MAKE THIS?!

"PRETTY SIMPLE, ACTUALLY! ON CHRISTMAS EVE, YOU JUST GET A CASSEROLE DISH AND PUT DOWN A LAYER OF BREAD--
I USED DAY-OLD WHITE BREAD WITH THE CRUSTS OFF.
CHEESE TRIO
BACK BACON
THEN YOU ADD A LAYER OF BACK BACON (MAKE SURE TO GIVE A LITTLE BIT TO ANY CHONKY BOIS LOITERING AROUND THE KITCHEN), A LAYER OF CHEDDAR, AND ANOTHER LAYER OF BREAD.
BREAD
NEXT YOU TAKE 6 EGGS, 3 CUPS OF MILK, 1/4 CUP OF MINCED ONIONS, SOME SALT AND PEPPER, AND A TEASPOON EACH OF WORCESTERSHIRE, TABASCO, AND DRY MUSTARD AND MIX IT ALL UP IN A BOWL.
P
S
3×
CUP
WORCESTIRE SAUCE
TABASCO
YOU POUR THAT MIXTURE OVER THE BREAD, MEAT, AND CHEESE; COVER IT UP; AND STICK IT IN THE FRIDGE!

BREAD
CHEESE
BACK BACON
SO, JUST A BIG HAM AND CHEESE SANDWICH, THEN.
UH, WOW, I NEVER THOUGHT OF IT LIKE THAT, BUT...YEAH! EXACTLY!
CLEANUP CREW
ON CHRISTMAS MORNING, YOU POUR A 1/2 CUP OF MELTED BUTTER ON TOP AND COVER THE WHOLE THING WITH A BUNCH OF SMASHED-UP CORNFLAKES!
CORNFLAKES
THEN YOU JUST CHUCK IT IN THE OVEN AT 350 FOR AN HOUR, AND BOOM!
SIMPLE, TASTY CHRISTMAS BREAKFAST!"
NOT BAD, MIKE. NOT BAD AT ALL.
WIPE WIPE
DEEDLE DEET!

OH! IT'S HAZEL!
HI, HAZE! MERRY CHRISTMAS! DID YOU OPEN YOUR PRESENTS YET?

HI, MINDY!
NOT ALL OF THEM, BUT I JUST GOT TO THE ONE YOU GAVE ME!

THANKS SO MUCH FOR THE AWESOME SHIRT!
IT ALMOST LOOKS LIKE SCRAPS!!

HAHA! YOU'RE WELCOME!
I HAD TO ORDER IT ONLINE. IT ALMOST DIDN'T COME IN TIME!
DID YOU LIKE WHAT I GOT YOU?

SORRY! WE HAVEN'T OPENED ANYTHING YET EXCEPT FOR STOCKINGS!

AH!! HERE'S YOURS!
OPEN IT!

GASP

IT'S SCRAPS!!
YEAH!!
I MADE IT OUT OF MODELING CLAY AND PAINTED IT!!

HAZEL, THIS IS AMAZING!
THANKS! I MADE ONE FOR EVERYONE!

GROAN
I CAN'T BELIEVE I JUST BRAGGED TO YOU ABOUT ORDERING YOUR GIFT ONLINE!

HAHA! DON'T FEEL BAD! I JUST LIKE MAKING STUFF!
WELL, IT'S AWESOME.
THANKS!

DEEDLE DEET!
HANG ON. I'M GETTING ANOTHER FACECHAT, BUT I DON'T RECOGNIZE THE NUMBER.
BLOOP!

HEY!

GABBY?
WHOSE PHONE ARE YOU CALLING FROM?
IT'S MINE!!
WHAT?!
YOUR PARENTS FINALLY GOT YOU YOUR OWN PHONE?!

YUP!
IT'S THE BRAND-NEW PRO VERSION!
YOU SHOULD SEE THE SPECS ON THIS BABY! IT WAS JUST RELEASED LAST WEEK!

OF COURSE IT WAS. ONLY THE BEST FOR YOU.
LET'S LOOP PRIYA INTO THIS! HANG ON...

DEEDLE DEET!
HI, PRIYA!!
GUESS WHAT? I GOT MY OWN PHONE!

OH, THAT'S NICE...
NICE?
IT'S AH-MAZ-ING!!
D'YOU KNOW HOW LONG I'VE BEEN ASKING FOR ONE?

YEAH...

YEAH, GABS. WE ALL KNOW HOW LONG YOU'VE BEEN--
HEY, IS EVERYTHING OKAY, PRIYA?

YEAH, I...NO...

PRIYA?
WHAT'S WRONG?

BOXING DAY, DECEMBER 26
I CAN'T BELIEVE YOU'RE BEING EVICTED!
YOU HAVE TO MOVE?! THAT STINKS!!

AND THEY WAITED UNTIL JUST BEFORE CHRISTMAS TO TELL YOU?
THAT'S... THAT'S SO AWFUL!!

YEAH, THEY SAID THEY HAD TO GIVE US NOTICE BEFORE THE END OF THE MONTH AND THEY WERE GOING AWAY FOR THE HOLIDAYS, SO...

WHAT A ROTTEN THING TO DO!!
BUT WHY ARE THEY KICKING YOU OUT??
SOMETHING ABOUT RENOVATIONS?
DAD SAYS IT'S JUST AN EXCUSE TO GET RID OF US AND CHARGE THE NEXT RENTERS WAY MORE MONEY.

BUT I THOUGHT YOU ***OWNED*** YOUR HOUSE.

WHAT?
NO. WHY DID YOU THINK ***THAT?***
YEAH, GABBY. PRIYA ***RENTS,*** LIKE ME AND MY MOM.

WELL, ***I*** DON'T KNOW!
I GUESS I JUST ASSUMED, BECAUSE YOUR DAD IS A *DOCTOR--*
OMG, GABBY! MY DAD IS ***NOT*** A DOCTOR!

HE'S... NOT?
BUT I THOUGHT YOU ***SAID--***

GABBY, I'VE ***TOLD*** YOU! HE ***USED*** TO BE A DOCTOR BACK IN ***INDIA!***
BUT WHEN WE CAME TO CANADA, THEY WOULDN'T LET HIM BE ONE ***HERE!***

OH, THAT'S TERRIBLE! WHY WOULDN'T THEY LET HIM BE A DOCTOR?
SIGH I CAN'T REMEMBER. SOMETHING ABOUT... "CREDITATIONS" OR WHATEVER?

SO... WHAT DOES HE DO?
WELL, HE USED TO DO WHATEVER HE COULD WHILE HE WENT BACK TO SCHOOL. HE DROVE A TAXI FOR A WHILE...
BUT HE JUST GOT A NEW JOB WORKING IN A LAB AS A... TECH? I THINK?

I'M SORRY, PRIYA.
I GUESS I FORGOT.

IT'S OKAY.
ANYWAY, IT COMPLETELY RUINED CHRISTMAS.

MOM AND DAD HAVE BEEN OBSESSED WITH FINDING A NEW PLACE EVER SINCE WE FOUND OUT.
WE HAVE A COUPLE OF MONTHS BEFORE WE HAVE TO LEAVE, BUT MY DAD IS SO ANGRY HE WANTS OUT RIGHT AWAY.
ARF! ARF!!
?!

PICKLES! SCRAPS!
WHAT ARE YOU DOING?!!

GRRRR!

GRRR...
SCRAPS

!!

OMG!! SCRAPS!! LET GO!!

HA!HA! HA!
PICKLES!! PUT HIM DOWN!!

SHAKE!
SHAKE!

YIPE!!

OOF!!
PLP!
PMFF!

HUFF
HUFF
ARF!
HUFF

ARF!

HEH...
?!
SCRAPS

RRR...

SLIP!
!

?!
YIPE!!

NF!

ARF! ARF!

?

OOF!!

?!

HMF!

HA!HA! HA!
SCRAPS, YOU GOOFY LITTLE *MEATBALL!*

NO ONE WILL EVER *BELIEVE* THAT JUST HAPPENED!
SKRTCH
SKRTCH
PAT PAT

CAN YOU IMAGINE IF WE'D *RECORDED* THAT??
OH, MAN! THAT'D BE *EPIC!!*

UM... *GUYS?*

LATER...
HEY THERE, SWEET GIRL!
HOW WAS THE DOG WALKING TODAY?

HMMM?

DOG WALKING! I ASKED HOW IT WAS!
HONESTLY, GABBY! IT REALLY BOTHERS ME WHEN YOU'RE SO LOST IN YOUR PHONE THAT YOU DON'T HEAR--

DAD, I'M SORRY, OKAY?!
BUT YOU'LL NEVER BELIEVE WHAT I JUST FILMED! YOU HAVE TO WATCH THIS!

OH, WOW! THIS JUST HAPPENED?
SHH! WATCH TO THE END!

HAHA! UNREAL!!

GABBY, THAT'S AMAZING! CAN YOU SEND THAT TO ME?
HECK, YOU SHOULD POST THAT VIDEO TO THE PAWS PICTAGRAM ACCOUNT SO I CAN SHARE IT WITH YOUR AUNTIES AND NANA AND GRANDDAD.

YOU THINK SO?
FOR SURE!
YOUR MOM SENDS ME A LOT OF ANIMAL VIDEOS, AND THAT'S ONE OF THE BEST I'VE EVER SEEN!

YEAH, OKAY, MAYBE I WILL! I'VE NEVER POSTED BEFORE. THAT'S ALWAYS BEEN *MINDY'S* JOB.
HM...OKAY. I THINK...YEAH! THERE WE GO!

POSTED!
COOL, I'LL GIVE IT YOUR FIRST *LIKE!*

BZZT!
THANKS, DAD.

ALL RIGHT, IT'S GETTING LATE.
TIME TO PUT YOUR PHONE *AWAY* AND GET STARTED ON THAT *ASSIGNMENT* YOU'VE BEEN PUTTING OFF.
CHRISTMAS BREAK WILL BE OVER BEFORE YOU *KNOW* IT.

AWW, COME *ON,* DAD!
JUST A FEW MORE MINUTES?

GABBY, WE TALKED ABOUT THIS.
WE DIDN'T GET YOU THAT PHONE SO YOU COULD SIT AND STARE AT IT ALL NIGHT LONG.

WE'VE GOT DINNER AND THEN DISHES AND THEN I WANT YOU TO DO A PROPER PIANO PRACTICE.
UGH! FINE!

AND DON'T FORGET TO MUTE NOTIFICATIONS!
YEAH, YEAH...
GRUMBLE

THE NEXT MORNING
GABBY! BREAKFAST IS READY!!

URRGH, 'M COMIN'.

I STILL DON'T SEE WHY YOU HAD TO WAKE ME UP SO EARLY!

EARLY?! IT'S NINE THIRTY! YOU'VE BEEN ASLEEP FOR ALMOST TWELVE HOURS!

YEAH, BUT IT'S CHRISTMAS BREAK!
WELL, IT'LL BE OVER IN A WEEK AND YOU NEED TO GET BACK ON A REGULAR SLEEP SCHEDULE.

BUT SLEEPING IN FEELS GOOD!
DON'T YOU WANT ME TO BE HAPPY?

OF COURSE I DO!
AS EVIDENCE, OBSERVE THE PANCAKES AND BACON THAT I HAVE LOVINGLY PREPARED FOR YOU!
BUTTER MILK

OH, THAT SMELLS--
?

OH MY GOSH!

THIS IS SO COOL!
I KNOW!! FOUR HUNDRED LIKES! AND OVER FIFTY NEW FOLLOWERS!
JEEZ, YOU GUYS. RELAX!

IT'S NOT THAT BIG A DEAL. I MEAN, 400 LIKES ISN'T BAD...

...BUT I POSTED A SKATEBOARDING TOKTIK LAST YEAR THAT HAD OVER A THOUSAND LIKES AND SOMETHING LIKE 20,000 VIEWS.

YEAH, YEAH. SORRY TO BE EXCITED.
THE MOST LIKES PAWS HAS HAD BEFORE IS AROUND TWENTY!

MINDY, HOW MANY TOKTIK FOLLOWERS DO YOU HAVE?
I'M NOT SURE. HONESTLY, I'M KIND OF OVER SOCIAL MEDIA THESE DAYS.

OR MAYBE YOU'RE JUST SAYING THAT BECAUSE NONE OF YOUR PAWS POSTS WENT VIRAL.

NO WAY!
ALL I'M SAYING IS IT'S NOT A B--
IF YOU SAY "BIG DEAL" AGAIN...

I'M THROWING THIS BAGGIE OF DOG POOP AT YOU.
WHAT?!

YOU.
WOULDN'T.
DARE.

YOU ASKED FOR IT! HERE COMES TURDS!
AAHH! GABBY, STOP!!

AAHH!!
PRIYA! HELP!!
HAHAHA!!
HEY, GUYS.
WHAT'S...UH, HAPPENING?

PRIYA! THERE YOU ARE! HAVE YOU BEEN WATCHING GABBY'S POST? WE'RE DOING NUMBERS!
HUH? OH, SORRY. I SAW IT EARLIER, BUT I HAVEN'T BEEN WATCHING IT.

WHAT IS WITH YOU GIRLS??
I FINALLY GET MY OWN PHONE AND HAVE A HIT POST, AND YOU DON'T EVEN CARE!

HEY! I THINK IT'S COOL!!
IT IS COOL. ALL I'M SAYING IS THAT SOCIAL MEDIA DOESN'T ACTUALLY MEAN ANYTHING.

UGH, YOU SOUND JUST LIKE MY DAD. CAN I GET SOME MORE ENTHUSIASM, PLEASE, GIRLS?
SORRY. I'M JUST A BIT... DISTRACTED LATELY.
YEAH, I BET.

SO...HOW'S EVERYTHING GOING?
OKAY, I GUESS. THINGS ARE PRETTY HECTIC AT HOME.

ANY LUCK FINDING A NEW PLACE?
A BIT? MY DAD HAS BEEN LOOKING EVERYWHERE.
WE'RE GOING TO SEE A HOUSE THIS AFTERNOON, ACTUALLY.

OH... THAT'S GOOD, RIGHT?
MAYBE? DAD SEEMS TO THINK SO, ANYWAY.

IS IT CLOSE BY?
I DON'T THINK SO. DAD SAYS HE HASN'T SEEN A SINGLE THING AVAILABLE IN THIS NEIGHBORHOOD.

OH...

THAT AFTERNOON...
<SO, WHAT DID YOU THINK, KIDS? NOT BAD, RIGHT?>
<YEAH!>
<YEAH, IT'S COOL!>
<WHAT ABOUT YOU, PRIYA?
DON'T YOU THINK THE ROOM AT THE END OF THE HALL WOULD BE NICE FOR YOU?>
HUH? OH, YEAH. IT'S... FINE.
SWISH!
<DEAR, I THINK IT'S MORE THAN FINE.
IN A LOT OF WAYS IT'S BETTER THAN WHERE WE LIVE NOW.>
<COME ON, LET'S GO FOR A LITTLE WALK! I WANT TO SHOW YOU SOMETHING!>

<DO YOU KNOW THAT I COME TO THIS NEIGHBORHOOD ALMOST EVERY WEEK TO DO SOME OF OUR SHOPPING?>
<YOU *DO?*>
<*MM-HMM!* A LOT OF THESE SHOPS ARE THE ONLY PLACES IN TOWN THAT SELL WHAT WE NEED.>
PUNJABI MARKET
E51ST
Jewellers Inc.
NJ
Main
OPEN

<THIS STORE RIGHT HERE, FOR EXAMPLE, IS WHERE I GET ALL MY ***SPICES.***>
OPEN

<AND HERE IS WHERE I GOT ALL OUR NICE ***DRESSES*** FOR YOUR COUSIN'S WEDDING LAST SPRING!>

Himalaya Restaurant
<AND LOOK AT ALL OF THESE RESTAURANTS! THIS ONE MIGHT HAVE THE BEST VEGETARIAN BUFFET IN VANCOUVER!>
OH, I *REMEMBER* THIS PLACE!
6587
WELCOME
BUFFET

OOOH... A *MITHAI SHOP!*
SWEETS!!

WHY IS THERE SO MUCH *INDIAN* STUFF HERE?
THIS NEIGHBORHOOD IS KNOWN AS *PUNJABI MARKET* BECAUSE SO MANY INDIAN IMMIGRANTS BUILT HOMES AND BUSINESSES HERE.
TANDOORI OVEN

HUH. PRETTY *NEAT.*

IT'S JUST SO FAR FROM SCHOOL AND ALL OF MY *FRIENDS!*
CAN'T WE FIND SOMEWHERE *CLOSER?*

‹PRIYA, YOUR FATHER AND I SPENT THE LAST WEEK LOOKING *EVERYWHERE,* AND THIS IS BY FAR THE BEST PLACE WE'VE FOUND.
PLUS IT'S AFFORDABLE, AND IT'S AVAILABLE TO MOVE INTO RIGHT *NOW!*›
Straight

‹HONESTLY, WE FEEL REALLY, *REALLY* LUCKY TO HAVE FOUND THIS PLACE. I DON'T THINK WE CAN PASS IT UP.›

BUT... HOW AM I GOING TO GET BACK TO *BRONTË* EVERY DAY? ISN'T IT *WAY* TOO FAR TO WALK?

WELL, CHUTKI... I AM NOT SURE YOU *CAN.*
I THINK YOU WILL HAVE TO *LEAVE* BRONTË.
CAFE
WELCOME
OPEN

WH-WHAT?

‹THERE'S A WONDERFUL SCHOOL JUST THREE BLOCKS FROM HERE! WATTERSON ELEMENTARY!
AND ONLY A FEW BLOCKS PAST THAT IS ONE OF THE BEST HIGH SCHOO--›

NO! I'M NOT LEAVING BRONTË! YOU CAN'T MAKE ME!
PRIYA, I KNOW THIS IS HARD, BUT--

NO! I-I'LL GET UP AN HOUR EARLY EVERY DAY AND RUN, IF I HAVE TO! I'LL QUIT ALL MY SPORTS! I'LL TAKE THE BUS!

I'M NOT LEAVING MY FRIENDS!!

<THERE YOU ARE! I'VE BEEN LOOKING ALL OVER FOR YOU!
ISN'T IT WONDERFUL?! WHAT A RELIEF! I FEEL LIKE WE WON THE LOTT-->

EXCUSE ME.
HUH?
BMP!

<LITTLE GIRL, DON'T YOU WALK AWAY FROM ME! WE AREN'T FINISHED HERE!>
?

UH...
WHAT DID I MISS?

OMG, OMG, OMG! THIS IS AMAZING!
GABBY, WHAT DID WE TELL YOU TEN MINUTES AGO?
IT'S TIME TO PUT THAT PHONE DOWN FOR THE NIGHT.

ARE YOU KIDDING ME??
WE JUST HIT 5,000 LIKES ON THIS POST!

WAIT, SERIOUSLY? HOW DID THAT HAPPEN?
I THOUGHT YOU SAID THIS MORNING THAT IT TOPPED OUT AT 1,000 LIKES?

I DID! BUT IT WAS REPOSTED BY THIS BIG DOG ACCOUNT A COUPLE HOURS AGO, AND IT'S BLOWING UP AGAIN!

WELL, THAT'S GREAT, GABBY. WE'RE VERY HAPPY FOR YOU. BUT THAT DOESN'T CHANGE THE FACT IT'S PAST EIGHT. NO MORE SCROLLING TODAY.
BUT--

NO "BUTS," GABBY. I'M *SERIOUS.*
BUT *MINDY* DOESN'T HAVE LIMITS ON *HER* SCREEN TIME. WHY DO *I*--

GABBY, YOU KNOW THE ***RULES.*** DO NOT MAKE US REGRET GETTING YOU THIS PHONE!
UGH!

IT'S NOT ***FAIR!!***
SLAM!

GABBY!
STOMP!
STOMP!
STOMP!
OMP!

LATER THAT NIGHT...
11:01
HUMPH

11:02
GROAN

CLIK.

CRRRREEEEEAAK

RK
RK
RK
RK

CLIK.

FWUMP!

TAP!
TAP!
TAP!
TAP!
TAP!
TAP!
TAP!

DEF
HAPPY NEW YEAR
"THERE WE GO! HOLD *STILL,* BOY!"
SLOW-MO SQUARE PHOTO VIDEO PANORAMA
DEF
ZZZ...
KISS ME
"OKAY, YOU'RE HOLDING A BIT *TOO* STILL, SCRAPS."

DEF
"*ARGH!* JACK! QUIT *MOVING!!*"
SLOW-MO SQUARE PHOTO VIDEO PANORAMA

WHY ARE WE DOING THIS AGAIN?
I *TOLD* YOU, I STARTED A *TOKTIK* ACCOUNT FOR *PAWS* LAST NIGHT...
AND I WANT SOME NEW YEAR'S CONTENT FOR OUR FIRST POST!

LAST NIGHT? HOW DID YOU DO THAT?
I THOUGHT YOUR PARENTS DIDN'T LET YOU LOOK AT YOUR PHONE AT NIGHT.

NO. I CAN LOOK AT IT WHENEVER I WANT.
IT'S MY PHONE.

OKAYYY.
BUT WHAT MADE YOU JOIN UP IN THE FIRST PLACE?
I READ A THING ABOUT GROWING YOUR BRAND...
PAWS

...AND IT SAID THE BEST WAY TO, UM, GET MORE FOLLOWERS IS TO CROSS-PROMOTE YOUR STUFF ACROSS... AH...
ACROSS...

YAWN

...ACROSS LOTS OF PLATFORMS.
SEEMS LIKE A WASTE OF TIME, IF YOU ASK ME.

HEY!! I HEARD THAT! I PUT A LOT OF WORK INTO THIS AND THINK IT'S REALLY COOL!

WE'VE HAD AN ACCOUNT FOR MONTHS NOW, SO WHY IS IT SUDDENLY A WASTE OF TIME AS SOON AS I GET A PHONE?
THAT'S NOT FAIR!

SIGH
YOU'RE RIGHT, OKAY? I'M SORRY.

UGH!
IT'S THIS MOVE! I'VE BEEN SPENDING ALL MY FREE TIME HELPING MOM AND DAD PACK, AND I'M JUST... FRUSTRATED.
IT'S BAD ENOUGH THAT I HAVE TO LEAVE, BUT IT'S ALL HAPPENING SO MUCH FASTER THAN I'D EXPECTED.

IT REALLY IS!
YEAH! YOU TOLD US YOU'VE FOUND A NEW HOUSE...
BUT I THOUGHT YOU HAD A COUPLE OF MONTHS BEFORE YOU HAD TO MOVE OUT OF YOUR OLD PLACE!

WE DO, BUT THE NEW PLACE IS AVAILABLE ON THE FIRST OF JANUARY. DAD SAYS THE ONLY REASON WE CAN GET IT AT ALL IS BECAUSE WE'RE ABLE TO MOVE ON SUCH SHORT NOTICE.
PLUS, IF WE MOVE OUT EARLY, OUR OLD LANDLORD HAS TO PAY US A FULL MONTH OF FREE RENT.

OH. THAT'S PRETTY GOOD, RIGHT?
YEAH, I GUESS.
IT'S JUST SO STRESSFUL, AND SO MUCH WORK!

WELL, MAYBE IT'D BE A BIT LESS STRESSFUL IF WE HELPED YOU MOVE!
REALLY? YOU'D DO THAT?

YEAH, SURE! I BET MY MOM AND MICHAEL WOULD BE HAPPY TO HELP OUT.

MICHAEL'S SUPER STRONG! VERY HANDY FOR LIFTING HEAVY STUFF!
HAHA! MY DAD'S NOT VERY STRONG, BUT I BET HE'D HELP, TOO!

AW, I DON'T THINK DAD AND I CAN HELP.
WE'RE TAKING MY GRANDPARENTS TO VANCOUVER ISLAND ON THE FIRST.

EVERYONE IS STILL GOING TO BE ABLE TO COME OVER TOMORROW FOR MY NEW YEAR'S EVE PARTY, THOUGH, RIGHT?
OF COURSE!

ACTUALLY, I WAS GOING TO TELL YOU--THAT'S THE DAY BEFORE WE MOVE.
MOM SAYS WE'LL BE TOO BUSY ALL NIGHT.
OH. OKAY.

A-AND WHAT ABOUT AFTER?
AREN'T YOU WORRIED ABOUT SCHOOL? AND...PAWS?

AH, JEEZ. WHAT DO I SAY? "YES"? "ALL THE TIME"?
UM, I-I...

NAH, IT'S *FINE!!* I'M SURE IT WILL ALL WORK OUT!!

THERE'S NO WAY YOU GUYS ARE GETTING RID OF ME *THAT* EASILY!
NOW COME *ON!*

LET'S GET THIS GOOFY HAT ON *JACK!*

?!

OKAY, SURE. MAYBE THAT WAS A BIT *PHONY,* BUT THERE'S NO POINT BRINGING EVERYONE *ELSE* DOWN JUST BECAUSE *I'M* MISERABLE.
HAHAHA!
I WISH THIS WASN'T *HAPPENING...*

...BUT IT DOESN'T REALLY MATTER WHAT I WISH.
NEW YEAR'S EVE
I JUST HAVE TO DEAL WITH IT.

SIGH I CAN'T BELIEVE THIS IS MY LAST NIGHT IN THIS PLACE. IT'S THE ONLY HOME I'VE EVER KNOWN.
BRON

AND I KNOW IT'S JUST A HOUSE, BUT IT MAKES ME WONDER WHAT ELSE I'LL BE LEAVING BEHIND.
PAWS Stuff

MY SCHOOL, MY FRIENDS...PAWS.
PAWS
PRETTY AWESOME WALKERS
WE LOVE FLOOFS!
WE LOVE DOGGOS!
WE LOVE PUPPERS!
NEED YOUR DOG WALKED FROM 3-6 DURING THE WEEK? WE CAN HELP!
CALL US NOW!!

IT'S ALL JUST SO MUCH TO HANDLE.
PART OF ME IS GLAD I'M NOT WITH THE REST OF THEM RIGHT NOW.

NOT A VERY *BIG* PART, THOUGH.
THIS IS *IT,* PEOPLE! JUST A FEW MINUTES TILL MIDNIGHT!

EVERYONE NEEDS TO GET A DRINK AND A NOISEMAKER READY TO RING IN THE NEW YEAR!!

NOISEMAKERS, DAD? ARE YOU *SURE?*
HNY

ZZZ...
WHAT ABOUT NANA AND GRANDDAD?

THEM? KIDDO, I DON'T THINK WE COULD WAKE THEM IF WE *TRIED!* AND I PLAN TO TRY!

AW, COME ON! LESS THAN A HUNDRED LIKES ON TODAY'S POST? WHAT'S UP WITH THAT??
ARE YOU STILL WORRYING ABOUT THAT? IT'S NEW YEAR'S EVE!
YEAH, GABBY, LET IT GO! PUT YOUR PHONE DOWN!
HNY
SORRY. I JUST DON'T GET IT! WE'VE GOT ALMOST 500 FOLLOWERS NOW. WHY SO FEW LIKES?
BECAUSE NO ONE REALLY CAAAAARES?
HEY!
OH, LOOK! THEY'VE STARTED THE COUNTDOWN! COME ON, EVERYONE!
COUNTDOWN
10
FIVE!
FOUR!
THREE!
TWO!

WELL, THAT'S IT. A NEW DAY AND A NEW YEAR. EVERYTHING *CHANGES* NOW.
12:00
AND I ONLY WISH I COULD STOP THINKING THAT IT WON'T JUST BE *ME* WHO'S MOVING. ONCE I'M ALL THE WAY ON THE OTHER SIDE OF TOWN...

...WHAT'S TO STOP MY *FRIENDS* FROM MOVING ON WITHOUT M--

BRRM!
HUH?

GABBO
Happy New Year!
Hazel
HAPPY NEW YEAR! We miss you!
Mindy
HNY! Wish you were here! See you tomorrow!
I mean, later today, I guess, LOL!!

SNIFF

THE NEXT MORNING
HEY, THIS PLACE IS *NICE!*
YEAH, I ACTUALLY LIKE IT BETTER THAN YOUR *OLD* PLACE, I THINK!
604-VAN-MOVR
Call now for a quote!
VAN MOVERS

REALLY?
SURE! I MEAN, DON'T *YOU?*
PRIYA'S BOOKS
PRIYA'S TROPHIES

YEAH, I *GUESS...*

WELL, COME ON! LET'S CHECK OUT YOUR NEW ROOM!

YO! WHICH WAY TO PRIYA'S ROOM?!
UP THE STAIRS AND TO THE LEFT, MINDY!

WHOA!
LOOK HOW MUCH SPACE! COOL!
YEAH!

AH, IT JUST LOOKS BIG BECAUSE THERE'S NO FURNITURE.

NO WAY! LOOK! YOU CAN PUT YOUR BED RIGHT HERE AND STILL HAVE TONS OF ROOM!
MAYBE EVEN GET A BIGGER BED AND JUST STARFISH ALL NIGHT!
HOLY CATS!
IS THIS A CLOSET OR ANOTHER ROOM??
OH, COME ON. IT'S NOT REALLY THAT BIG.
CLIK!
IF YOU SAY SO.
I'VE NEVER SEEN A CLOSET WITH ITS OWN LIGHT SWITCH BEFORE, THOUGH!
HA, YEAH. YOU KNOW WHAT? I GUESS IT IS A PRETTY NICE ROOM!
NO GUESSING ABOUT IT! I THINK IT'S GREAT!

YEAH, PLUS THIS CARPETING IS LEGIT. I CAN DEFINITELY SEE MYSELF ZONKED OUT ON THIS BAD BOY AT MANY A SLEEPOVER.
OH, GABBY...
HAHA!

SPECIAL DELIVERY!
HUFF *PUFF*

GREAT JOB, BUD.
THANKS!
OH, BOY, HOW THE HECK AM I GONNA GET ALL THIS STUFF UNPACKED BEFORE SCHOOL STARTS AGAIN ON MONDAY?
SO, YOU'RE DEFINITELY COMING BACK, THEN? TO BRONTË?

YES! OF COURSE! I TOLD YOU!
I KNOW! I WAS JUST WORRIED!

OOF. I HAD SUCH A FIGHT WITH MY MOM OVER THIS. BUT SHE'S GONNA LET ME KEEP GOING TO BRONTË IF I TAKE THE BUS EVERY DAY AND PAY FOR IT WITH MY PAWS MONEY.

OH, THAT'S NOT A PROBLEM! PUBLIC TRANSIT IS FREE UNTIL YOU TURN TWELVE IN MARCH!

IT IS?!
HOW DO YOU KNOW THAT?
HOW DO YOU NOT KNOW THAT? ACTUALLY, WAIT, LET ME GUESS -- YOU'VE NEVER RIDDEN A BUS, HAVE YOU?

YES, I HAVE!
HOW MANY TIMES HAVE YOU RIDDEN ONE?

...TWICE.
HAHAHA! THAT'S MY GIRL!

H-HAVE YOU EVER TAKEN THE BUS... ALONE?
SURE, A FEW TIMES! IT'S FINE!

I MEAN, SOMETIMES PEOPLE ARE A LITTLE SMELLY OR GROSS, BUT LIKE... THAT'S JUST PEOPLE!
PEOPLE ARE SOMETIMES SMELLY AND GROSS!

YEAH!
LIKE LEO SHAUGHNESSY.

HAHA! HA!!
I LOVE HOW YOU WILL BE THAT KID'S ENEMY FOREVER.
BECAUSE HE'S THE WORST!

DID SOMEONE UP HERE ORDER A MATTRESS?
HAHA! ME! I DID!

LITTLE HELP HERE?? PLEASE??
OH, DAD! SERIOUSLY?!

WHAT?! THIS THING IS HEAVY!
HAHAHA!
SOMEHOW, MOVING DAY ENDS UP BEING KIND OF FUN! WE EAT PIZZA AND SAMOSAS, AND THEN GABBY'S DAD FALLS ASLEEP ON THE SOFA!
BY THE TIME I GO TO BED THAT NIGHT, I ACTUALLY FEEL OKAY ABOUT EVERYTHING.

UNFORTUNATELY, THAT FEELING ONLY LASTS UNTIL *MONDAY MORNING.*
ALL RIGHT, MOM! I'M GONNA GO TO *SCHOOL* NOW!

‹OKAY! I'LL WALK YOU TO THE *BUS STOP!*›
KITCHEN

MOM, IT'S ONLY LIKE TWO BLOCKS *AWAY.*
I'LL BE *FINE.*

OKAY, DEAR. IF YOU ARE SURE. HAVE A NICE--
BYE!
SLAM!

DAY.

OKAY, I ADMIT THAT WAS PRETTY RUDE OF ME. BUT IT'S BAD ENOUGH SHE MOVED ME ALL THE WAY ACROSS TOWN.
I DON'T WANT HER HOLDING MY HAND AT THE BUS STOP AND EMBARRASSING ME AS WELL!

I JUST HOPE THAT MINDY'S RIGHT AND TAKING THE BUS ALONE ISN'T A PROB--

OH, JEEZ.

WHAT IS GOING ON HERE? SHOULD I BE STANDING BEHIND THIS GUY?

IS THAT GUY EVEN WAITING FOR THE BUS? WHY ISN'T THERE A PROPER LINE?!

OKAY, OKAY...
HERE WE GO!
AR!! . . . HAPPY N
BOOP!
THEY'RE ALL SWIPING THEIR CARDS! *UGH!* WHY COULDN'T THERE BE SOME OTHER KIDS GETTING ON SO I CAN SEE WHAT TO *DO??*
I SHOULD HAVE ASKED *MINDY* ABOUT THIS!!

DO I JUST GET *ON?* DO I NEED TO *SAY* SOMETHING?
YOU GETTING *ON?*
UM... YEAH.

I'M ONLY ELEVEN.
I-IT'S FREE FOR *ME,* RIGHT?

BEHIND THE LINE, PLEASE.

HUH?
GOTTA BE BEHIND THE LINE.

OH! OKAY!

HEY!
BMP!

LOOK OUT, KID.
SORRY! SORRY!

AWW, MAN.
THIS THING IS *PACKED!*

WHERE ARE ALL THESE PEOPLE *GOING?*

WOULD YOU LIKE TO *SIT?*
OH! UH, THANKS.

HOW DO PEOPLE DO THIS *EVERY DAY?*

BRRRRIIIIIINNNGGGG!!
"WHERE IS SHE?"

THAT WAS THE LAST BELL!
THE MORNING ASSEMBLY IS ABOUT TO START!
EXIT

YOU DON'T SUPPOSE THAT SHE CHANGED HER MIND ABOUT SWITCHING SCHOOLS?
NO! SHE WOULDN'T DO THAT!
I DON'T THINK...

UGH!
IT'S SO ANNOYING THAT I CAN'T JUST TEXT AND ASK HER WHERE SHE IS!!

SO YOU'RE REALLY NOT ALLOWED TO USE YOUR PHONE AT SCHOOL?

NO. MY DAD PUT ALL THESE PARENTAL CONTROLS ON IT.

LIKE, WHAT AM I SUPPOSED TO DO IF I NEED TO LOOK SOMETHING UP IN CLASS?? OR IF THERE'S AN EMERGENCY?
OH!!
BANG!

THERE SHE IS!!
HUFF PUFF

SORRY I'M *LATE,* MS. MIRANDA!
WHAT HAPPENED?

I HAD TO TRANSFER BUSES AND THE SECOND BUS WAS *LATE.* AND THEN I DIDN'T REALIZE HOW *FAR* THE FINAL STOP IS FROM SCHOOL!
IT'S LIKE A *TEN*-MINUTE WALK AWAY!
IT TOOK ME ALMOST *AN HOUR* TO GET HERE TODAY!!

THANK YOU FOR YOUR *ATTENTION,* AND WELCOME BACK, BRONTË!
I HOPE YOU ALL HAD A *WONDERFUL* HOLIDAY.
EEP!

I'D LIKE TO START WITH AN ACT OF RECONCILIATION AND ACKNOWLEDGE THAT WE LIVE, WORK, AND PLAY ON THE UNCEDED TRADITIONAL TERRITORIES OF THE MUSQUEAM, SQUAMISH, AND TSLEIL-WAUTUTH NATIONS.

NOW, BEFORE WE GET STARTED WITH OUR GUEST SPEAKERS, I'D LIKE TO OPEN UP THE FLOOR.
IF YOU'RE A TEACHER AND HAVE AN ANNOUNCEMENT THAT YOU'D LIKE TO SHARE, PLEASE ***STAND*** WHEN MY HAND COMES TO YOU.

YES, ***MS. MIRANDA?***

THANK YOU, PRINCIPAL SINGH! ***HI, EVERYONE!*** I JUST WANTED TO SHARE A FUN LITTLE STORY ABOUT A FEW LOCAL ***CELEBRITIES*** WITH YOU ALL!

I WAS LOOKING AT MY PHONE LAST NIGHT AND SAW SOMETHING AMAZING.
I'M SURE YOU ALL KNOW THE AUK? IT'S THE BEST ANIMAL-RELATED ACCOUNT ON THE WHOLE INTERNET!

ANYWAY, I WAS WATCHING THE FUNNIEST LITTLE DOG VIDEO, AND THEN I SAID, "HOLD ON, IS THAT MY SCHOOL IN THE BACKGROUND?"
AND SO I CLICKED THROUGH AND DISCOVERED THAT IT WAS FILMED BY SOME OF MY OWN STUDENTS!

GABBY JORDAN, PRIYA GUPTA, MINDY PARK, AND HAZEL MILLER!

IT TURNS OUT THAT THESE GIRLS RUN A DOG-WALKING BUSINESS CALLED PAWS!
ISN'T THAT JUST GREAT? LET ME TELL YOU...
HEH HEH...

AFTER SCHOOL...
SEE YOU TOMORROW, GUYS!
BYE, HAZE!

HAVE FUN AT PHYSIO!

HEH! "FUN"?
PHYSIOTHERAPY ISN'T EXACTLY "FUN," GABBY.

AGH!
I MEAN, HAVE A GOOD TIME--
NOPE.
I MEAN, ENJOY--
JUST STOP.
I MEAN... JUST...
BYE!

HAHA!
OKAY, BYE, GABBY!

"HAVE FUN."
AUGGH...
HAHA HA!

HAHA HA!
HI, GIRLS! WHAT'S SO FUNNY?
OH, NOTHING, DAD.
I'M JUST A HUGE GOOF, IS ALL.
OH, OKAY! COOL!

ANYWAY, HOW ABOUT THAT ASSEMBLY THIS MORNING? WASN'T IT GREAT?
I THOUGHT IT WAS KINDA... EMBARRASSING.
NO WAY! I HAD PEOPLE COMING UP TO ASK ME ABOUT THE VIDEO ALL DAY.
PAWS

ABOUT THE VIDEO OR ABOUT PAWS?
THE VIDEO! THEY ALL WANTED TO KNOW THE NAME OF OUR ACCOUNT SO THEY COULD FOLLOW US.

HOW MANY NEW FOLLOWERS DID WE GET?
PRIYA'S

I DUNNO!
MY PHONE JUST UNLOCKED LIKE A MINUTE AGO.
I CHECKED AT LUNCH AND WE HAD LIKE FORTY NEW FOLLOWERS ALREADY.
NO IDEA HOW MANY WERE FROM BRONTË, THOUGH!

OKAY, LET'S SEE. OH, COOL! CHLOE IS FOLLOWING US NOW, AND SEBASTIEN! SLOANE AND PEYTON, AND--
OH, NO. IT CAN'T BE.

WHAT?
WHO ELSE IS FOLLOWING US?

IT'S TOO HORRIBLE. I CAN'T EVEN SAY IT.
OMG! LEO IS FOLLOWING US??

I'M GONNA BLOCK HIM.
GABBY, NO!
HAHA! HA!

OKAY, FINE! LISTEN, LET'S TALK ABOUT OUR SOCIAL MEDIA STRATEGY! WE NEED TO FIND A WAY TO KEEP DRIVING ENGAGEMENT.

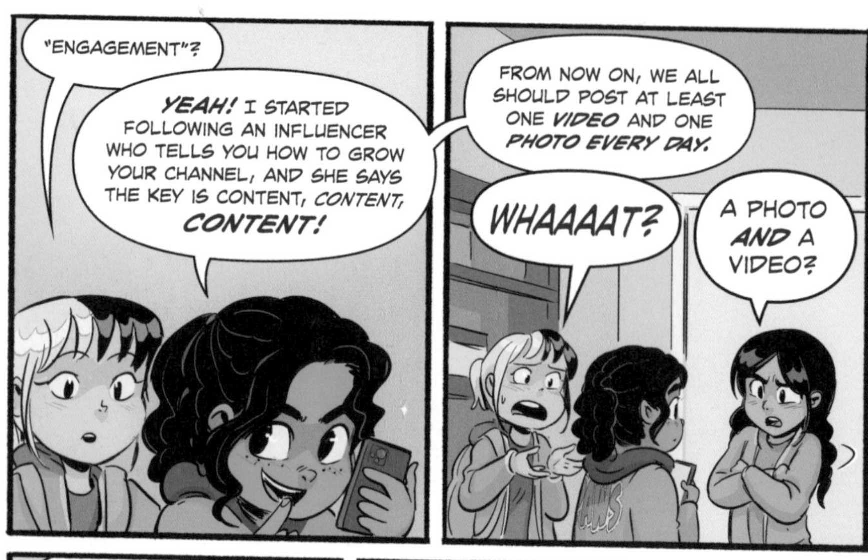
"ENGAGEMENT"?
YEAH! I STARTED FOLLOWING AN INFLUENCER WHO TELLS YOU HOW TO GROW YOUR CHANNEL, AND SHE SAYS THE KEY IS CONTENT, CONTENT, CONTENT!
FROM NOW ON, WE ALL SHOULD POST AT LEAST ONE VIDEO AND ONE PHOTO EVERY DAY.
WHAAAAT?
A PHOTO AND A VIDEO?

YEAH! AND WE NEED TO BE SMARTER ABOUT MUSIC CHOICES! ONE OF US SHOULD ALWAYS BE USING WHATEVER THE TOP AUDIO TRACK IS THAT DAY.
OH, COOL--
HOMEWORK.
OH! AND SHE SAYS WE NEED TO MAKE SURE WE'RE EDITING OUR PHOTOS BEFORE POSTING! PUNCH THOSE LEVELS! BOOST SATURATION!

GABBY, I REALLY DON'T HAVE TIME FOR THIS.
I'VE GOT TO CATCH A BUS TO SOCCER PRACTICE THE SECOND I FINISH MY WALK OR I'LL BE LATE.

WHY ISN'T YOUR MOM COMING TO *DRIVE* YOU?
I THINK SHE'S UPSET WITH ME FOR REFUSING TO CHANGE SCHOOLS, AND ALL THIS BUSING IS HER WAY OF MAKING A *POINT.*

JEEZ...
THAT SUCKS, PRIYA. I'M SORRY.

YEAH.
THAT'S *ROUGH.*

ANYWAY, WE CAN'T ALL JUST POST AT THE SAME *TIME.* WE NEED TO SPACE THEM *OUT.* SO WE'LL HAVE TO WORK OUT A *SCHEDULE--*

UGH! I'M OUT OF HERE. I'VE GOT A DOG TO WALK. THERE'S NO *TIME!*

OMG, WOULD YOU JUST *RELAX?* IT'LL BE *FINE!!*

OF COURSE, IT WASN'T FINE.
BY THE TIME I WALKED PICKLES AND CHANGED INTO MY SOCCER UNIFORM BACK AT GABBY'S, I WAS ALREADY RUNNING BEHIND.
AND THEN I HAD TO WASTE TEN MINUTES TALKING ABOUT A "POSTING SCHEDULE" BEFORE I COULD ESCAPE!
COACH JANEY! I'M HERE!
PRIYA! SO NICE OF YOU TO FINALLY JOIN US!
SORRY! I'M SORRY! THE BUS WAS SO FULL IT DIDN'T EVEN STOP, AND I HAD TO WAIT FOR--
I'M REALLY NOT INTERESTED IN HEARING EXCUSES, PRIYA.
YOU'RE GONNA HAVE TO WARM UP AND STRETCH DOUBLE TIME IF YOU WANT TO JOIN IN THE REST OF TODAY'S DRILLS.
OKAY, I'M SORRY. IT WON'T HAPPEN AGAIN!

IT BETTER NOT.
NOW GET YOUR CLEATS ON AND GIVE ME THREE LAPS OF THE FIELD.
THREE? OKAY...

SIGH
FLUMP

CAN THIS DAY POSSIBLY GET ANY WORSE?
DING!
FWEEE!
HUH?

Hey, Priya! Just saw that you haven't posted anything from today's walk yet! Don't forget!
BAR
HYDRATE

UGH! LAY OFF, GABBY! JUST BECAUSE YOU HAVE NOTHING ELSE GOING O--

PRIYA!
EEP!

WHY ARE YOU JUST SITTING THERE LOOKING AT YOUR PHONE?!
NOW IT'S SIX LAPS AROUND THE FIELD! LET'S GO!!
GROAN

AAARGH! IF THIS IS HOW JUST THE FIRST DAY BACK AT SCHOOL IS GOING...
HOW AM I SUPPOSED TO KEEP THIS UP?!

THE NEXT WEEK

BAH!
8:22 AM
Time Limit
You've reached your limit on Pictagram
OK

MORNING, GABBY!

FINALLY! SOMEONE'S HERE! QUICK! CAN I USE YOUR PHONE?

UH, SURE. WHAT'S *UP*?
AHH, DAD WOULDN'T LET ME LOOK AT MINE THIS MORNING, AND NOW IT'S *LOCKED* UNTIL AFTER SCHOOL!

I'M DYING TO SEE HOW EVERYONE'S POSTS ARE DOING! OUR LIKES AND VIEWS HAVE BEEN DROPPING ALL WEEK!
OKAAAYY.

UGH! *TERRIBLE!*
WHAT IS?

PRIYA'S POST YESTERDAY! IT'S DONE ALMOST *NO* NUMBERS!
I THOUGHT IT WAS *CUTE!*

ARE YOU *KIDDING?* ONLY *TWO* LIKES?
WE SHOULD *DELETE* IT!

ISN'T THAT KIND OF...*MEAN?*
NO! IT'S BRAND MANAGEMENT! I READ A *THING* ABOUT IT!
YOU SHOULD DELETE LOW-ENGAGEMENT POSTS SO YOUR PAGE LOOKS MORE *SUCCESSFUL!*

REALLY? BECAUSE YOU AND PRIYA HAVE BEEN BICKERING A LOT LATELY.
NO! I'D BE DOING THE SAME IF IT WAS MY OWN POST!

HEY.
GAH!
!

PRIYA! HI!
HI, PRIYA! WE WERE JUST TALKING ABOUT YOU!

YOU WERE? WHAT WERE YOU SAYING?

NOTHING! HAHA! NOTHING AT ALL!
ARE YOU OKAY? YOU LOOK EXHAUSTED.

URRHHHH. I AM. I MISS LIVING RIGHT NEXT TO THE SCHOOL AND BEING ABLE TO SLEEP INNNNN!

CAN I MOVE INTO YOUR GARAGE?
PLEEEEASE?!
WHOA!

I'LL BE EVER SO QUIET. YOU WON'T EVEN KNOW I'M THERE.
I'LL BE LIKE A LITTLE ITTY-BITTUMS MOUSEY MOUSE.

HAHA! ARE YOU LEGIT OKAY?
SIGH I THINK THE LACK OF SLEEP IS GETTING TO ME.

OKAY, ANYWAY, I'VE BEEN THINKING ABOUT OUR "EVERYONE POST SOMETHING EVERY DAY" POLICY, AND I THINK WE SHOULD TRY A NEW PLAN.
HUH? WHAT--

I SAY WE SHOULD ALL FILM SOMETHING EVERY DAY, BUT WE TAKE TWENTY MINUTES AT THE END OF EVERY WALK BACK AT HQ TO COMPARE OUR VIDEOS AND POST ONLY THE BEST CONTENT FROM EACH DAY.

TWENTY MINUTES? I ALMOST NEVER GET HOME IN TIME FOR DINNER AS IT IS! THE BUSES ARE PACKED AND TAKE FOREVER AT THAT TIME OF DAY!

YEAH, BUT I REALLY THINK THIS IS BEST FOR ENGAGEMENT--
GABBY, I FEEL LIKE I'M DROWNING. I LITERALLY COULDN'T CARE LESS ABOUT SOCIAL MEDIA RIGHT NOW.

YOU-- I...

WELL, I... WELL, MAYBE I DON'T CARE ABOUT BUS SCHEDULES!
HEY, GUYS! WHAT'S U--

WHOAAA!!
WHAT ARE THESE VIBES??

THESE ARE BAD VIBES!

ACK! NO! THE VIBES, THEY...
THEY ARE TOXIC.

OKAY, MINDY-- WE GET IT.
HAHA!
TELL MY MOM... I LOVE HER.
TELL MICHAEL...

...HE'S...
A DORK.

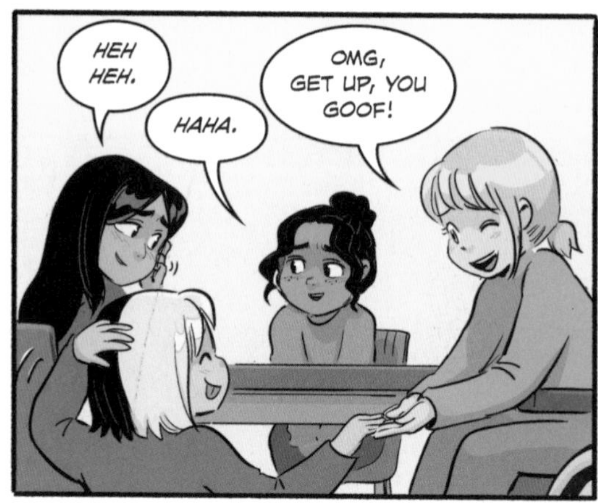
HEH HEH.
HAHA.
OMG, GET UP, YOU GOOF!

GABBY AND I MANAGE NOT TO BITE EACH OTHER'S HEADS OFF FOR THE REST OF THE DAY, BUT I JUST DON'T SEE WHY SHE--

HEY! HEADS UP!
HUH?
BMP!

SORRY ABOUT THAT! GOT AWAY FROM ME!
HEY, TAKE A SHOT!

OKAY...

SWSH!

WHOA!
NICE FORM! LACED IT!
HA, THANKS!

YOU PLAY?
A BIT. I WAS ON MY SCHOOL TEAM LAST YEAR.

HEY, I KNOW YOU, DON'T I? YOU JUST MOVED IN ACROSS THE STREET FROM ME, RIGHT?
UH, YEAH, I THINK SO. DO YOU LIVE IN THAT GREEN HOUSE WITH THE GARAGE?
THAT'S HER! AND I'M JUST DOWN THE BLOCK.

UM, THIS IS GOING TO SOUND ODD, BUT...DO YOU GO TO BRONTË ELEMENTARY?
UH, YEAH! HOW DID YOU KNOW THAT?

YOU SEE? I TOLD YOU IT WAS HER!
YEAH, YEAH, OKAY.

SORRY. UM, WE JUST RECOGNIZED YOU BECAUSE YOU KICKED OUR *BUTTS* IN THE DISTRICT TRACK MEET LAST YEAR.
UM, EX*CUSE* ME! SHE KICKED *YOUR* BUTT. *I* ALMOST HAD HER!

OH! I REMEMBER YOU GUYS!
YOU GO TO THAT SCHOOL WITH THE *ORANGE* UNIFORMS, RIGHT?

THAT'S *US!* I'M *SIMRAN!*
I'M PRIYA!
KIARA.
DAP!

WAIT, IS *THIS* YOUR SCHOOL?
YEAH! WATTERSON!
OH, COOL! YOU ALWAYS HAVE THE *BEST* TRACK TEAMS.

THANKS! YEAH, THE SPORTS PROGRAM IS REALLY GREAT HERE.
WELL, *MOSTLY.* OUR BASKETBALL TEAM IS GOING TO BE *LOUSY* THIS YEAR.

AH, WE WON'T BE *THAT* BAD. WE JUST NEED A BETTER SHOOTING GUARD THAN *LAST* YEAR!

HEY! SHAYLA WAS ALL RIGHT!
COME *ON!* SHAY WAS NICE AND ALL, BUT SHE HAD *NO* HANDLES AND EVERY TIME SHE GOT A SHOT OFF IT WAS AN ABSOLUTE *BRICK.*

HAHA! *HARSH!*
JUST KEEPING IT *REAL,* IS ALL.

HEY, YOU WANT TO HANG OUT AND HOOP A BIT, PRIYA?
AGH, I'D LIKE TO, BUT I SHOULD GET GOING. LATE FOR DINNER.

AH, THAT'S OKAY. IT'S GETTING DARK, ANYWAY.
COOL IF WE *WALK* WITH YOU?
SURE!

DING!

GABBO >
not really sure ab
Just Now
Delive
Hey, P -- I just spotted a couple typos in today's post. Make sure to check your spelling before you post to the account! Thaaaaaaaaanks !
uMessage

UGH!
YOU GOOD?

YEAH, IT'S NOTHING. JUST... A KID IN MY CLASS.
READY WHEN YOU ARE!

HUH? WHY DID I SAY THAT? GABBY'S NOT JUST SOME KID IN MY CLASS! SHE'S BEEN ONE OF MY BEST FRIENDS SINCE FOREVER!

IT'S JUST... SHE REALLY *IS* GETTING ON MY NERVES WITH ALL THIS SOCIAL MEDIA STUFF.
I *GET* IT. IT'S COOL TO HAVE HUNDREDS OF PEOPLE LIKE OUR POSTS AND SAY NICE THINGS! *OBVIOUSLY!*

BUT, LIKE, I'VE GOT A *LOT* ON MY PLATE RIGHT NOW, AND THAT DOESN'T SEEM TO *MATTER* TO HER AT ALL.
WHY CAN'T SHE *SEE* THAT? DOESN'T SHE *CARE?*
WHY DOESN'T SHE THINK ABOUT *ME* FIRST, FOR A CHANGE?
PAWS
Pretty_Awesome_WalkerS
Pretty_Awesome_WalkerS Looking fresh in our new bandanas!!!!! #Stylin #BANDANARAMA
Post
Add a comment...

DOES IT MATTER TO HER THAT I HAVE TO TRUDGE TO A BUS STOP AFTER EVERY DAY OF DOG WALKING?
SURE DOESN'T SEEM LIKE IT!
Pretty_Awesome_WalkerS
Pretty_Awesome_WalkerS Roxy lets u know when you're not throwing the ball enough!
Add a comment...
Post
DOES ANYONE CARE THAT I MISS DINNER WITH MY FAMILY HALF THE TIME? BEATS ME!
I CAN BARELY KEEP MY EYES OPEN IN CLASS MOST DAYS, AND, LIKE...DOES ANYONE EVEN NOTICE??

I KNOW, I KNOW! IT'S NOT *FAIR* TO BE MAD AT THEM.
IT'S NOT LIKE IT'S *THEIR* FAULT THAT I MOVED ALL THE WAY ACROSS THE CITY.

Pretty_Awesome_WalkerS
Pretty_Awesome_WalkerS Can't get enough of our sweet and salty Pickles. #OG_DOG
Post
Add a comment...

BUT I'M WORKING SO *HARD* TO KEEP EVERYTHING THE SAME AT SCHOOL AND AT *PAWS* BECAUSE I DON'T WANT TO *RUIN* WHAT WE'VE GOT!
I'M DOING ALL OF THIS FOR *THEM!*
AREN'T I?

SIGH I DON'T KNOW. I'M JUST *TIRED.*
TIRED OF CHANGE. TIRED OF *FIGHTING* CHANGE.

AND AS THE DAYS GO BY, I'M STARTING TO FEEL LIKE MAYBE BY FIGHTING SO HARD TO KEEP EVERYTHING THE SAME, THE THING THAT'S CHANGING THE MOST IS ME.
THE THINGS THAT I LOVE, THAT ALWAYS BROUGHT ME SO MUCH JOY, NOW FEEL LIKE A BURDEN.
BRONTË BASKETBALL TRYOUTS!!
GIRLS: Feb 2, 3:30-5:30
BOYS: Feb 2, 3:30-5:30
Sign up at the OFFICE
LIKE THINGS I HAVE TO DO.
Pretty_Awesome_WalkerS
Pretty_Awesome_WalkerS Scraps just absolutely crushin' his puppacino!
Add a comment...
Post
I'M NO QUITTER. I TRY TO WIN EVERY CHALLENGE I TAKE ON. BUT I HAVE TO ADMIT THAT THIS IS A FIGHT I FEEL LIKE I'M LOSING.
AND MORE THAN THAT...
Z Z Z

...IT'S A FIGHT THAT I'M NOT EVEN SURE I ***WANT*** TO WIN ANYMORE.
SEE YA *TOMORROW,* GUYS!!

SIGH

HEY, PRIYA?
HM?

HOW...HOW ARE YOU DOING?

ME? OH, I'M OKAY.
REALLY?

I...WELL, NO. I GUESS NOT REALLY.
THIS LAST MONTH HAS BEEN...SUPER HARD.

IT WAS HARD TO MANAGE BOTH SCHOOL AND SPORTS BEFORE THE MOVE...
BEFORE WE EVEN STARTED PAWS, HONESTLY.
BUT NOW? I JUST DON'T KNOW HOW MUCH LONGER I CAN KEEP IT UP.

OH.
I CAN'T HELP FEELING LIKE IT'S PARTLY MY FAULT.

WHAT? NO!
WHY DO YOU THINK THAT??

REMEMBER THE VERY FIRST TIME WE WALKED PICKLES? AFTER? IN YOUR OLD ROOM?

YOU WEREN'T SURE WE COULD HANDLE MORE THAN ONE DOG, AND GABBY AND I, WE JUST...WE JUST IGNORED YOU?
OH, YEAH.

BUT YOU WERE RIGHT!
I'M GLAD WE GOT MORE DOGS!
I CAN'T IMAGINE IF I'D NEVER MET SCRAPS AND ROXY AND THE REST!

WELL, I'M STILL SORRY.
AT THE VERY LEAST, I SHOULD TALK TO GABBY AND GET HER TO BACK OFF ON ALL THE SOCIAL MEDIA STUFF.
YEAH, MAYBE.

SHE'S REALLY GOTTEN CARRIED A...A...AH--

AH--CHOO!!

SNIFF
WHOA! ARE YOU OKAY?

BLECH. YEAH, JUST A SCRATCHY THROAT. I'M GOOD.
WELL, ANYWAY, DON'T WORRY ABOUT ME.
I'M SURE IT'LL ALL BE BETTER IN THE MORNING.

I HOPE SO!
SNIFF
SEE YOU TOMORROW, PRIYA!
BYE!

2535

PRIYA!

MOM?
HELLO, CHUTKI!

WHAT ARE YOU--
MFF
DOING HERE?

SIGH
<I AM WORRIED ABOUT YOU. AND ALSO, I AM SORRY.>
<SORRY? FOR *WHAT?*>

<SORRY FOR ***MANY*** THINGS.
SORRY THAT WE HAD TO MOVE. SORRY FOR NOT MAKING ALL OF THIS *EASIER.*>

OH.

‹THE THING IS, AS PROUD OF YOU AS I AM, I WORRY THAT YOU ARE *PUSHING* YOURSELF TOO MUCH.›

‹YOU'RE... *PROUD* OF ME?›

‹OF *COURSE!*
I AM PROUD THAT YOU WORK SO *HARD.*›
‹I AM PROUD THAT YOU REFUSE TO *QUIT!*
IT'S *REMARKABLE!*›

‹I WANT TO LET YOU MAKE YOUR OWN CHOICES. BUT YOU ARE STILL SO *YOUNG* AND THINK YOU CAN DO *EVERYTHING.*›

YEAH, IT'S A LOT HARDER THAN I THOUGHT IT'D BE. SO MUCH HAS *CHANGED...*

CHANGE IS THE LAW OF THE UNIVERSE, MY LOVE.

AS THE GITA SAYS, TO BE WISE IS TO ACCEPT CHANGE.
TO BE ENLIGHTENED IS TO LOVE IT.

WHOA!
SOUNDS LIKE SOMEONE'S BEEN GOING TO TEMPLE!

HUMPH <JUST BECAUSE WE RARELY GO TO TEMPLE DOESN'T MEAN I DON'T PAY ATTENTION WHEN I AM THERE!
PERHAPS YOU SHOULD TRY IT SOMETIME!>

HAHA!
<OKAY, MOM. WHATEVER YOU SAY...>

LATE THAT NIGHT AT GABBY'S HOUSE...

Liked by MWJordan and 1 other
Add a comment
BAH!

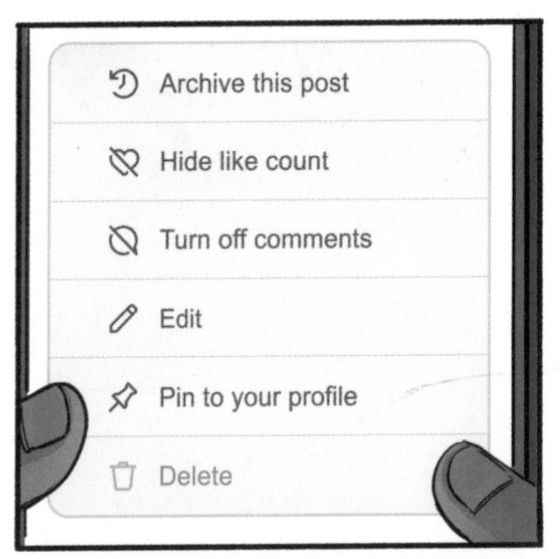
Archive this post
Hide like count
Turn off comments
Edit
Pin to your profile
Delete

Delete Post?
Deleted posts will be saved for 30 days before being permanently deleted
Delete
Cancel

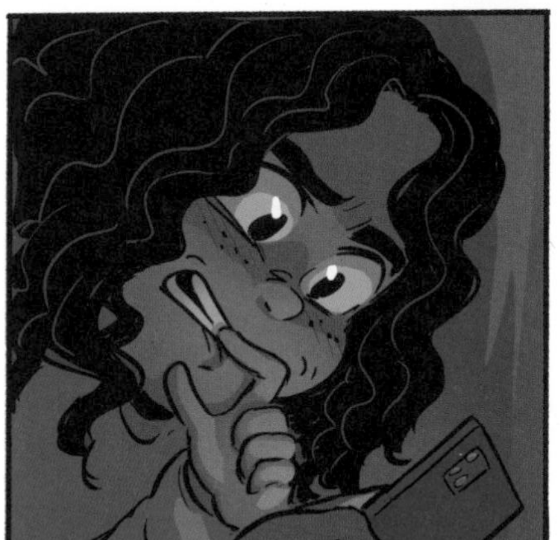

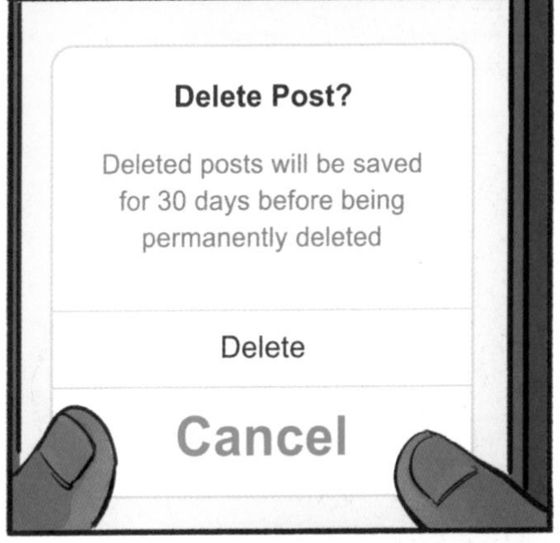
Delete Post?
Deleted posts will be saved for 30 days before being permanently deleted
Delete
Cancel

HUH?
11:22 PM
Time Limit

LOCKED OUT?
WHAT DO YOU MEAN? HOW??

AHEM

CLIK!
EEP!

UH-OH.
I THINK WE NEED TO HAVE A SERIOUS TALK, YOUNG LADY.

THE NEXT MORNING
BEEP
BEEP
BEEP

URHHH.
BLINK
BLINK

HUH?
WHY IS IT SO--

OH, WOW!

KNOCK!
KNOCK!
HUH?

PRIYA?
ARE YOU *AWAKE?*

HEY, MOM. I'M UP.
I GUESS I SHOULD LEAVE A BIT *EARLY* TODAY. THE BUS IS GOING TO BE A ***NIGHTMARE.***
<ACTUALLY, THAT'S WHAT I WANTED TO TELL YOU...>

<I JUST HEARD ON THE RADIO...>
<SCHOOL IS ***CANCELED*** TODAY!>

DING!
HUH?

6:34 AM
KEVIN (Carl's Dad) >
Hi, Priya! I know you were going to walk Carl today, but today's job was called off because of all this snow, so I can walk him myself. Why don't you take the day off?

YES!

AHHH...

HOURS LATER...
ZZZZ...
DING!

?

Happy Snow Day!!
lol, same to you!!
can you FaceChat now?
sure--call me

BRRM! BRRM!
HEYYYY-ZEL!
HAHA! ARE YOU STILL IN BED? DID I WAKE YOU UP?

MM. YUP! LIVING THE DREAM, GURL.
JEEZ, I'M SORRY TO BOTHER YOU, BUT I'VE GOT A PROBLEM AND CAN'T REACH GABBY.
SHE'S NOT ANSWERING ANY OF MY TEXTS OR DMS!

I'VE BEEN LOOKING OUT THE WINDOW ALL MORNING AND WE'RE THE *ONLY* HOUSE ON THE WHOLE STREET THAT'S CLEARED OUR *SIDEWALK.*

OH, NO!
YEAH, I GUESS IT SNOWS SO *RARELY* HERE THAT PEOPLE DON'T KNOW THEY'RE SUPPOSED TO *DO* THAT?

ANYWAY, THERE'S NO *WAY* I CAN GET AROUND OUT THERE. MINDY AND I WERE SUPPOSED TO TAKE DODY TO THE *VET* TODAY.
CAN YOU MAYBE DO IT *FOR* US?

OH, JEEZ... CAN'T MINDY DO IT ON HER *OWN?*

NO, THAT'S THE *PROBLEM!* MINDY TEXTED ME FIRST THING THIS MORNING TO SAY SHE WAS UP ALL NIGHT WITH A *FEVER* AND A *COUGH.*
SHE'S *SICK!*

FUMP!!
HUH?!

HEY, NEIGHBOR!!
HEY! WHAT ARE YOU GUYS DOING DOWN THERE?!

WE'RE TAKING SIMRAN'S LITTLE SISTER DOWN TO THE PARK!
WANNA COME? YOU CAN BRING YOUR BROTHERS, IF YOU WANT!
MY MOM EVEN GAVE ME SOME MONEY FOR HOT CHAI OR COCOA AFTER!

OH, WOW! I...I--
PRIYA?

WHAT'S GOING ON?
SIGH

IT'S NOTHING.
OKAY, SURE-- I CAN TAKE DODY FOR YOU.

OH, GREAT! ARE YOU SURE? IF IT'S A PROBLEM, I CAN KEEP TRYING GABBY? OR MAYBE EVEN ASK HER DAD?
NO, IT'S FINE. I CAN DO THIS. BYE.

SOON...

Mindy
mean lolol
hey Mindy sorry to bother u but I'm rly worried. I've been waiting at this stop for like an hour and there's still no bus

is there any chance your feeling better? LMK!!
ZZZZ...

FINALLY!
?!

KEEP MOVING BACK, PEOPLE! MAKE SPACE!

AH, MAN! COME ONNN!!
VRRRR!!
SSHHHHH!!

WHAT'S GOING ON?
UNBELIEVABLE!

SORRY, FOLKS. WE'RE STUCK.
THIS BUS ISN'T GOING ANYWHERE.

GREAT! NOW WHAT ARE WE SUPPOSED TO DO?!

GABBO
yo, Gabbo Gabbo! Why aren't you answering??
Are you seeing these texts? I really need to talk to you!!
hullILLLOOOOOOO??

BAH! GABBY, HOW DARE YOU FORCE ME TO USE THE PHONE AS A PHONE?

THAT'S IT, GIRL.
ALMOST THERE. HOLD STILLL...

BRIIING!!!
ARF!!
AAH! NO!

HELLO?! WHY ARE YOU CALLING ME, PRIYA?
CRUNCH! CRUNCH!

I'M CALLING BECAUSE YOU HAVEN'T ANSWERED ANY OF MY TEXTS!

UGH, SORRY. MY PARENTS HAVE COMPLETELY DISABLED EVERYTHING ON MY CELL EXCEPT PHONE CALLS "FOR EMERGENCIES"!
I CAN STILL ACCESS THE CAMERA THROUGH THE CONTROL PANEL, BUT I DON'T THINK THEY KN--

GABBY, I DON'T HAVE TIME FOR THIS!
I REALLY NEED YOU TO GO TO MEI'S AND PICK UP DODY.

WHAT?? I THOUGHT HAZEL AND MINDY--
MINDY IS SICK AND HAZEL IS STUCK AT HOME BECAUSE OF THE SNOW!

OH, I DIDN'T KNOW...
I'M TRYING TO COVER FOR THEM, BUT THE BUSES--

PRIYA, I GOT CAUGHT SNEAKING MY PHONE LAST NIGHT AND NOW I CAN'T EVEN TOUCH IT UNLESS I'M WALKING A DOG.
I HAVE TO FILM SOMETHING NOW, OR ELSE--

BLOOP.
HUH?

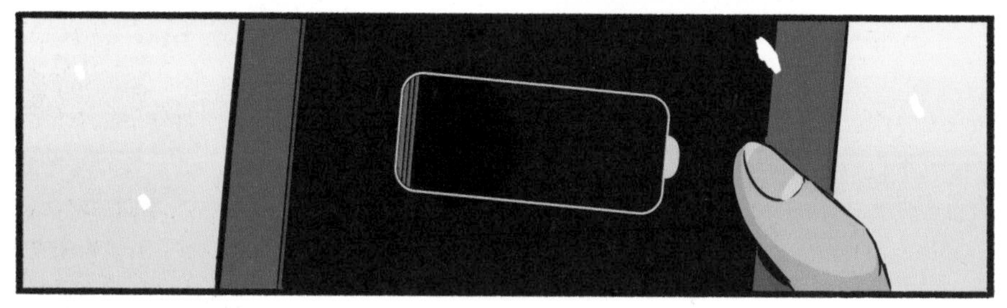

NOOOO!!

HELLO?
PRIYA? ARE YOU STILL *THERE?*

"CALL ENDED"?
PRETTY RUDE.

WELL, OKAY THEN-- I GUESS SHE DOESN'T NEED MY HELP, AFTER ALL!
COME ON, GIRL! LET'S GET THIS ***SHOT!***

Do Not Disturb
Sleep
NO MORE *INTERRUPTIONS!*

WHAT THE HECK AM I SUPPOSED TO DO *NOW?*
I NEED TO BE AT MEI'S PLACE IN TWENTY MINUTES AND IT'S AN HOUR-LONG WALK FROM HERE!

I GUESS I'LL JUST HAVE TO *RUN.*

I'M *GOOD* AT RUNNING.
I'M GOOD AT FIGHTING, AND *NOT GIVING UP.*

THIS IS JUST ANOTHER CHALLENGE.
ANOTHER *OBSTACLE* IN MY PATH.

WHEN THINGS LIKE THIS HAPPEN, I JUST NEED TO TRY HARDER, THAT'S ALL.

HAZEL NEEDS ME!
MEI NEEDS ME!
THEY ALL NEED ME!

EVEN GABBY NEEDS ME, IF SHE COULD JUST PULL HER HEAD OUT OF HER PHONE LONG ENOUGH TO SEE IT!

THIS IS NOTHING.
I CAN DO THIS.
I CAN MAKE IT!

I CAN--
AH!
SHHHHHHSH!!
SLAM!
UNH...
OOF...
WHA--

ARGHH!

I CAN'T DO THIS ANYMORE.

AHNN...

OOH.
AH!
OW!
OUCH...

MUCH LATER...
DAD! I'M HOME!
I KNOW YOU SAID TO BE BACK BY FOUR, BUT--

UM, DAD?
ARE YOU HOME?
CLICK!

DAD?
PRIYA?!

HEY.

WHY DON'T YOU HAVE A SEAT AT THE TABLE, PRIYA? I'LL GO GET THE FIRST AID KIT.
FIRST AID?

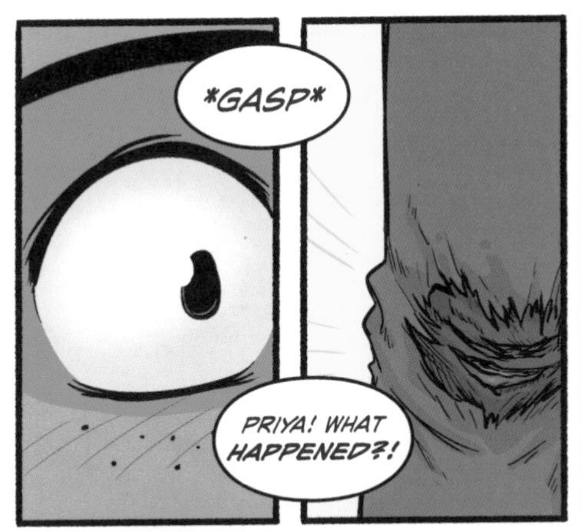
GASP
PRIYA! WHAT HAPPENED?!

WELL, AFTER --OW!-- MY PHONE DIED, I TRIED TO RUN, BUT ALL THE SNOW AND ICE WAS AWFUL, AND I TOTALLY WIPED OUT.

OH, NO! I...BUT, DOES THAT MEAN THAT DODY DIDN'T GET TO HER APPOINTMENT?
AND HOW DID YOU END UP HERE?

ACTUALLY, THAT WAS ME.

"WHEN PRIYA DIDN'T SHOW UP ON TIME TO WALK DODY TO HER APPOINTMENT, MEI CALLED ME. SHE WAS RATHER UPSET.
I TRIED TO CALL YOU, GABBY, BUT YOUR PHONE WENT STRAIGHT TO VOICE MAIL.
EEP!
SO I HOPPED IN THE CAR AND DROVE OVER TO MEI'S.
WHICH WAS A BAD IDEA, IT TURNED OUT.
I GOT STUCK ON THESE SIDE STREETS. MY FAULT, I GUESS. I DON'T HAVE WINTER TIRES.

I HAD TO BEG A COUPLE OF STRANGERS FOR A PUSH!

WE GOT TO THE VET LATE, SO I HAD TO *WAIT* UNTIL THEY COULD FIT US IN.
CUT-CLEAN-TRIM
GROOMING SPECIALS!

ANYWAY, I *FINALLY* GOT OUT OF THERE--
*YOU SHOULD SEE THE **MESS** DODY'S MUDDY PAWS MADE OF THE CAR SEAT, BY THE WAY.*

I DROPPED HER BACK HOME AND TOLD MEI WHAT THE VET SAID...
!

...AND THEN WHO SHOULD I MEET THERE, BUT ***PRIYA?***"
MALCOLM?

JEEZ, DAD, I'M *REALLY* SORRY.
WE'LL TALK ABOUT IT *LATER,* GABBY. RIGHT NOW I JUST WANT TO BE SURE PRIYA IS *OKAY.*

OH, PRIYA, ARE YOU--
DOES IT *HURT?*

NOT SO MUCH ANYMORE.
IT'S PRETTY MUCH JUST SORT OF *NUMB* NOW.

M-MAYBE IT'S NOT SO *BAD,* AFTER ALL.
I'LL TRY TO PULL UP MY PANT LEG AND TAKE A LOOK.
A-AHH!

OOOH, OUCH, OW! IT'S STICKING!
OMG.

OOF. THAT LOOKS PRETTY DEEP. YOU'LL PROBABLY NEED A STITCH OR TWO IN THERE.
OTHERWISE, IT'LL TAKE FOREVER TO HEAL AND LEAVE AN UGLY SCAR.

HOW ABOUT WE GET IT CLEANED UP, AND WHEN YOUR MOM GETS HERE WE CAN FIGURE OUT WHERE TO GO TO GET YOU ALL STITCHED UP?
SNIFF O-OKAY.

OH, PRIYA. I'M SO SORRY. I-I DIDN'T THINK...

IT'S OKAY-- OOH!
SORRY.

BUT...YOU WON'T BE ABLE TO PLAY SOCCER WITH YOUR LEG LIKE THAT!

HA, DON'T WORRY.
THERE PROBABLY WON'T BE ANY SOCCER FOR A WHILE WITH ALL THIS SNOW.
WSSHHH...

THIS IS ALL MY FAULT! I WAS SO FOCUSED ON OUR PICTAGRAM ACCOUNT AND MY DUMB PHONE THAT I DIDN'T REALIZE YOU NEEDED ME!!

YEAH...YOU HAVE GOTTEN KINDA OBSESSED WITH THAT STUFF.
YES, SHE HAS.

I'M GOING TO DELETE ALL OF OUR ACCOUNTS.

WHAT?!
ISN'T THAT KIND OF... DRASTIC? THEY'RE NOT JUST YOUR ACCOU--

I'M SICK OF THEM! THEY'RE ALL I CAN THINK ABOUT!
I DON'T SLEEP! I'M MORE FOCUSED ON GETTING LIKES THAN WALKING OUR DOGS!
EVEN MY GRADES ARE SLIPPING!

WAIT, WHAT?
I KNOW, DAD!
OKAY?!
I KNOW!

YOU WERE RIGHT! YOU WERE ALL RIGHT! THERE'S ABSOLUTELY NOTHING GOOD THAT HAS COME FROM THESE ACCOUNTS!
I WANT TO GET RID OF THEM!

GABBY, STOP. JUST...WAIT.
THE WHOLE TIME I WAS SLIPPING AND SLOGGING ACROSS THE CITY TO GET HERE, I WAS THINKING: WHAT IF THERE WAS SOMETHING WE COULD DO ABOUT IT?

SNIFF WHAT DO YOU MEAN?

WELL, WE'VE GOT ALL THESE FOLLOWERS NOW, RIGHT?
WHAT IF INSTEAD OF JUST TRYING TO GET LIKES FOR THE SAKE OF LIKES...
WE TRIED TO SHARE SOMETHING THAT'S ACTUALLY POSITIVE AND HELPFUL?

O-OKAY. THAT SOUNDS GOOD...
BUT WHAT DO YOU HAVE IN MIND?

A FEW DAYS LATER
OKAY! IS EVERYBODY READY?
YEP!
READY!

OKAY! ACTION!

HEY, THERE! I'M HAZEL, AND THIS LITTLE MAN ON MY LAP IS SCRAPS!

I'M A MEMBER OF PAWS, A GROUP OF DOG WALKERS IN VANCOUVER, CANADA!
Pretty_Awesome_WalkerS
Add a comment...
Post

THESE ARE SOME OF OUR PUPPOS! THIS IS *CORPORAL WAGS!*
Pretty_Awesome_WalkerS
Add a comment...
Post

AND THIS LITTLE BUNDLE OF ENERGY AND FARTS IS *CHAMPION JACK!*
Pretty_Awesome_WalkerS
Add a comment...
Post

AND THIS GORGEOUS MONSTER IS *PICKLES!*
Pretty_Awesome_WalkerS
Add a comment...
Post

ALMOST EVERY DAY AFTER SCHOOL, WE TAKE THESE GOOD BOYS AND GIRLS FOR FUN WALKS AROUND OUR NEIGHBORHOOD!
Pretty_Awesome_WalkerS
Add a comment...
Post

"BUT, HAZEL--ISN'T IT HARD TO USE YOUR WHEELCHAIR IN ALL OF THAT *SNOW??*"
Pretty_Awesome_WalkerS
Add a comment...
Post

GOOD QUESTION!
Pretty_Awesome_WalkerS
Add a comment...
Post

YES! IT'S *SUPER* HARD FOR ME TO GET AROUND! *AND NOT JUST ME!*
Pretty_Awesome_WalkerS
Add a comment...
Post

ALL *KINDS* OF PEOPLE, LIKE THE ELDERLY AND FOLKS WITH MOBILITY ISSUES, FIND IT CHALLENGING TO GET AROUND ON SNOWY SIDEWALKS!
Pretty_Awesome_WalkerS
Add a comment...
Post

AND, HECK, ANYONE CAN SLIP ON ICY SIDEWALKS!
Pretty_Awesome_WalkerS
Add a comment...
Post

DON'T BELIEVE ME? CHECK THIS OUT!!
Pretty_Awesome_WalkerS
EW!
CENSORED!
GROSS!
Add a comment...
Post

NOW, YOU MIGHT BE THINKING "THAT SURE SEEMS DANGEROUS," AND "THERE SHOULD BE A LAW ABOUT CLEARING YOUR SIDEWALKS."
Pretty_Awesome_WalkerS
Add a comment...
Post

AND THAT'S JUST THE THING--
Pretty_Awesome_WalkerS
Add a comment...
Post

THERE IS!!
Pretty_Awesome_WalkerS
Add a comment...
Post

TRAFFIC BYLAW 2849, SECTION 76, STATES "THE OWNER OR OCCUPIER OF ANY PARCEL OF REAL PROPERTY SHALL, NOT LATER THAN 10:00 A.M. EVERY DAY, REMOVE SNOW AND ICE FROM ANY SIDEWALK ADJACENT TO--"
Pretty_Awesome_WalkerS
Add a comment...
Post

OKAY, THAT'LL *DO*, DAD!
BUT I'M NOT *FINISHED!* THERE ARE TWO MORE *SUBSECTIONS!*
Pretty_Awesome_WalkerS
Add a comment...
Post

HAHA! SO, AS YOU CAN SEE, NOT ONLY IS CLEARING THE SIDEWALK OF SNOW A SUPER HELPFUL THING TO DO...
Pretty_Awesome_WalkerS
Add a comment...
Post

...IT'S THE LAW.
Pretty_Awesome_WalkerS
Add a comment...
Post

SO! FOR ALL YOUR NEIGHBORS ON TWO FEET, FOUR FEET, OR FOUR WHEELS, PLEASE DO THE RIGHT THING!
CLEAR YOUR WALKS!
Pretty_Awesome_WalkerS
Add a comment...
Post

THANKS A LOT!
Pretty_Awesome_WalkerS
Add a comment...
Post

RUFF!!
Pretty_Awesome_WalkerS
this message is
SCRAPS
APPROVED
Add a comment...
Post

AAAND POSTED!
YES!!
SWEET!

YOU'RE SURE YOU TAGGED THE CITY AND THE MAYOR, LIKE MY MOM SUGGESTED?
I'LL JUST CHECK.

OMG, GABS, YOU SAW HER DO IT!
STOP OBSESSING!

OKAY, OKAY, YOU'RE RIGHT! I'M SORRY! I DON'T KNOW WHY THIS STUFF GETS TO ME LIKE THIS.

IT'S OKAY, GABBY. WE GET IT.
ALL THAT STUFF--BLOWING UP, GOING VIRAL--CAN REALLY GO TO YOUR HEAD, ESPECIALLY AT FIRST.

YEAH! AND IF THIS POST GOES VIRAL, WE MIGHT ACTUALLY HELP SOME PEOPLE!

THANKS, GUYS. I HOPE SO, BUT I MOSTLY JUST WANT THINGS BACK TO NORMAL.
NO MORE OBSESSING. NO MORE RULES ABOUT POSTING EVERY SINGLE DAY.

NO MORE DELETING POSTS BECAUSE THEY DON'T GET ENOUGH LIKES?
OOF, YEAH. DEFINITELY NOT.

IF IT'S NOT FUN, THEN THERE'S NO POINT DOING IT, RIGHT?
RIGHT!

SO, WE'RE ALL GOOD, THEN?
OF COURSE!
UM...

ACTUALLY, UM, *ABOUT* THAT...
T-THIS IS SO HARD TO SAY, BUT...

...I'VE DECIDED TO...*CHANGE SCHOOLS.*
I START AT WATTERSON IN A *WEEK.*

WH-WHAT?

HEY, GIRLS! GREAT WORK TODAY! WHO WANTS *COCOA?!*

UH...

I'LL JUST LEAVE THIS HERE.
THANKS, DAD.

SO...YOU'RE SURE ABOUT THIS?
SIP

YEAH. ALL THE HOURS OF BUSING EVERY WEEK ARE KILLING ME.
MY SCHEDULE WAS ALREADY A MESS, BUT NOW...
I JUST FEEL LIKE I'M LETTING EVERYONE DOWN ALL THE TIME.

NO WAY, PRIYA!
WE DON'T THINK--
GUYS, YOU MIGHT NOT THINK IT, BUT IT'S HOW I FEEL.

A-AND FOR A WHILE I ALSO FELT KINDA MAD BECAUSE IT SEEMED LIKE NONE OF YOU WERE THINKING OF ME FIRST.

BUT I HATED FEELING THAT WAY! AND THAT'S WHEN I REALIZED THAT WASN'T YOUR JOB. I NEEDED TO PUT MYSELF FIRST.

A-AND MAYBE I CAN KEEP THIS UP UNTIL THE END OF THIS SCHOOL YEAR, BUT NEXT YEAR WOULD BE MY LAST AT BRONTË, AND AFTER THAT I'LL BE GOING TO A NEW SCHOOL NO MATTER WHAT!

A-AND, IT'S LIKE MY MOM SAYS-- I WAS ONLY LOOKING AT THE BAD SIDES, BUT NO CHANGE IS ALL GOOD OR ALL BAD. A-AND...

SIGH
...AND WHETHER I ASKED FOR IT OR NOT, THINGS HAVE CHANGED.
I THINK IT'S TIME FOR ME TO ACCEPT THAT.

UGH! I'M EXPLAINING THIS SO BADLY! I JUST... I NEED TO DO THIS, A-AND, AND...
I HOPE YOU ALL UNDERSTAND?

GUYS?
COME ON-- PLEASE SAY SOMETHING.

HONESTLY, PRIYA, I JUST CAN'T BELIEVE IT.
WH--

I CAN'T BELIEVE IT TOOK YOU THIS **LONG!**
HAHA! ***RIGHT?!***

WHAT?!

YOU... ***KNEW*** I WAS GOING TO DO THIS?
HOW COULD WE ***NOT*** KNOW?
ARE YOU *KIDDING?*
IT'S BEEN OBVIOUS FOR WEEKS THAT *SOMETHING* HAD TO GIVE!

YOU COULDN'T KEEP FALLING ASLEEP IN CLASS...
MISSING PRACTICES...
GETTING HOME LATE FOR DINNER!

THE REAL KICKER FOR ME WAS THE DAY YOU TOLD ME YOU WERE THINKING OF NOT JOINING THE BRONTË BASKETBALL TEAM THIS YEAR.
I WAS LIKE, *"WHO THE HECK **IS** THIS KID AND WHAT HAS SHE DONE WITH **PRIYA??**"*

OH, JEEZ. I REALLY HAVEN'T BEEN PAYING ATTENTION.

SO...YOU DO UNDERSTAND?
IF IT WERE ME, I'D HAVE ALREADY DONE IT!
OF COURSE!

JUST THINK! YOU CAN SLEEP IN FOR LIKE AN EXTRA HOUR EVERY DAY!
MMM... SLEEP!
YOU'LL DEFINITELY HAVE WAY MORE TIME FOR YOUR SPORTS!
I DO LOVE MY SPORTS!
HAHA! AND YOU MIGHT EVEN MAKE SOME NEW FRIENDS!

I DON'T LOVE THAT PART.

HA!HA!HA!

BUT... WHAT ABOUT *PAWS?*

I DON'T KNOW.
IT BREAKS MY *HEART* TO THINK OF NOT SEEING THE DOGS ANYMORE.

WELL, HOW ABOUT BECOMING A *CASUAL* MEMBER?
OH, LIKE, WHEN YOU'RE *FREE?* ON DAYS OFF, AND WEEKENDS AND STUFF? COULD YOU MAYBE DO *THAT?*
YEAH! JUST A COUPLE TIMES A MONTH?

I...
I'D *LOVE* THAT.

GREAT! IT'S SETTLED!
LET'S GO BACK INSIDE AND LOOK AT OUR *SCHEDULE!*

AND...LIKE, JUST BECAUSE I'LL BE AT A DIFFERENT SCHOOL...
IT DOESN'T MEAN WE CAN'T...STILL BE BEST FRIENDS, RIGHT?

I AM NOT EVEN *ANSWERING* THAT QUESTION.

NO *MORE SILLY QUESTIONS TODAY!*
HAHA! HA!
WE'RE ***DONE*** WITH THE SILLY QUESTIONS!

THE NEXT FEW WEEKS GO BY IN A BLUR. OUR POST ABOUT CLEARING SIDEWALKS BLOWS UP EVEN BIGGER THAN OUR FIRST VIRAL VIDEO!
THE OFFICIAL ACCOUNT FOR THE *CITY* EVEN REPOSTS IT!

WE ACTUALLY GET A CALL FROM THE ***MAYOR'S*** OFFICE ABOUT IT!
THEY WANT TO MEET US AND FILM A ***FOLLOW-UP*** POST!
UVER CITY HALL

THE LOCAL RADIO STATION EVEN ASKS TO ***INTERVIEW*** SOME OF US!

BUT SOCIAL MEDIA FAME IS A LOT LIKE SNOW IN VANCOUVER.
IT DOESN'T HAPPEN VERY OFTEN, AND WHEN IT DOES, IT DOESN'T STICK AROUND.

BEFORE YOU KNOW IT, THE NOTIFICATIONS HAVE DRIED UP, AND THE SIDEWALKS ARE CLEAR ONCE MORE!

AS FOR ME, I FEEL LIKE I CAN *BREATHE* AGAIN.
I'M EVEN ENJOYING BEING AROUND TO HELP MOM WITH *DINNER!*
FLOUR

OF COURSE, I MISS MY FRIENDS, BUT WE TEXT OR TALK *EVERY DAY,* AND I STILL MAKE SURE I SEE THEM WHENEVER I CAN.
PAWS

BEST OF ALL, I MANAGE TO GO ON A *PAWS* WALK ALMOST EVERY WEEK!
PAWS
PAWS

I WON'T LIE TO YOU--GETTING STARTED AT THE NEW SCHOOL HASN'T BEEN *EASY.*
I FELT LIKE I WAS GONNA *THROW UP* ON THE FIRST DAY!

FOR A WHILE THERE, I EVEN STARTED TO WONDER IF I'D MADE A *MISTAKE.*
BUT I STUCK *WITH* IT. I PUT MYSELF *OUT* THERE.

AND EVERY DAY GETS A BIT BETTER THAN THE *LAST.*

CHANGE IS *SCARY.*
AND IT'S *NATURAL* TO RESIST IT, TO HOLD ON TO THE THINGS YOU LOVE.

BUT CHANGE ALSO BRINGS NEW OPPORTUNITIES. NEW *POSSIBILITIES.* DIFFERENT, MAYBE EVEN *BETTER,* THAN WHAT YOU HAD BEFORE.
GIRLS
Basketball
TRYOUTS!!

YOU CAN'T SPEND YOUR LIFE FIGHTING CHANGE. (BELIEVE ME, I *TRIED!*) EVENTUALLY, YOU HAVE TO ACCEPT IT.
AND ONCE YOU DO THAT, YOU MIGHT COME TO *LOVE* IT!

YOU MIGHT END UP WONDERING WHY YOU BOTHERED TO FIGHT SO LONG AND HARD *AGAINST* IT.
PAWS

AND, WHO *KNOWS*--YOU MAY EVEN START TO WONDER IF THERE ARE *MORE* CHANGES THAT YOU'D LIKE TO MAKE!

...TELLING YOU, GUYS. WE ARE GONNA KICK SO MUCH *BUTT* THIS SEASON!
BET! WITH PRIYA AS OUR NEW ***TWO,*** WE'LL BE *UNSTOPPABLE.*

HAHA! ***EASY,*** GIRLS! WE DON'T EVEN KNOW IF I'M A *STARTER* YET!
OH, ***PLEASE!*** YOU SHOULD HAVE *SEEN* COACH WATCHING YOU AT TRYOUTS. I *GUARANTEE--*
B-LOOP!

OH, IT'S A TEXT FROM ***GABBY!***

4:30 PM
GABBO
be putting up our fliers tomorrow after school!!
Today 4:30 PM
Hey, P! check out the pics we just posted!!
Pretty Awesome WalkerS on Pictagram:
"OMG, Pickles! This dog is CRA...

CLICK THE LINK!
YEAH, LET'S SEE IT!

Pretty_Awesome_WalkerS
IS THAT PICKLES?
YEP!
Add a comment...

HAHA HA!
SWIPE!
Add a comment...
Post

OH, GREAT! NOW I'M HUNGRY FOR ICE CREAM!
SAME!

Aw! Miss them BOTH! Wish I was there!
TIK TEK TEC

Us, too!! 😭😭
I think Roxy misses your throwing arm the most!!
lol!! you just need to practice! You'll get stronger! 💪

4:34 PM
Priya!
stronger! 💪
Gotta go, Gabs! TTYL!! ❤
See you this weekend!!
Can't wait!!!! L8R!!

GABBY! COME ON!
DON'T MAKE US TAKE THAT THING AWAY FROM YOU!!

SORRY! SORRY!
I WAS JUST TEXTING PRIYA!

YO!
PRIYA!
GET A HUSTLE ON!

COMING!
YOU READY TO DO THIS?

YOU KNOW IT!

HOW'S THAT?
PERFECT!

PAWS
PRETTY AWESOME WALKERS
हम कुत्तों से प्यार करते हैं!
WE LOVE DOGGOS!
NEED YOUR DOG WALKED FROM 3-6 DURING THE WEEK? WE CAN HELP!
अपने कुत्ते को हफ्ते मे 3-6 बार सैर करवाना चाहते हैं? हम मदद कर सकते हैं!
CALL US NOW!!

PAWS 604-555-0826
PAWS 604-555-0826
PAWS 604-555-0826
PAWS 604-555-0826
PAWS 604-555-0826
PAWS 604-555-0826
PAWS 604-555-0826
PAWS 604-555-0826
PAWS 604-555-0826
PAWS 604-555-0826
PAWS 604-555-0826

ਮਾਰਕੀਟ
THE END!
(AND THE BEGINNING!)

Acknowledgments

Thank you to my family, Adam, Kiki, and Nicko, for the love, belief, and motivation to keep me drawing.

A very special thank-you to OneSpace—an amazing co-working space dedicated to working mothers. Without your resources, support, and community, this book would not be finished.

Thank you to Nathan for steering the ship and writing such heartfelt stories that I know will resonate with everyone.

Thank you to all the parents and young readers who have personally expressed their appreciation for our series. The series continues because of you! —M. A.

As always, I'd like to thank my wife, Rachel. She's been a tireless cheerleader of PAWS (and my career, in general) from the beginning. She makes everything easier.

I'd like to thank my partner, Michele, for continuing to surprise and delight me with her work on this series. I feel so grateful to have been able to watch her become an author and a mother. I know well how hard those jobs are, and the way she's managed to balance and excel at both of them is truly inspiring to me.

I'd like to thank everyone who has helped us get these books into the hands of our readers at schools, libraries, bookshops, book fairs, book clubs, and conventions across the world. Without the support of booksellers and librarians, none of our work would mean anything, because no one would ever see it!

I'd like to thank Mariyam Fatima for her kindness and for sharing her Hindi expertise with me.

Lastly, I'd like to thank all of our wonderful readers. We're so glad you like our books, and every time we get to meet you or hear from you, it means the world to us and fills us with excitement and energy to keep telling these stories for years to come! —N. F.

THE GIRLS OF

PAWS

WILL RETURN!